I0731614

tiny shifts

Kristian Himmelstrup

Translated from the Danish by
Nina Sokol

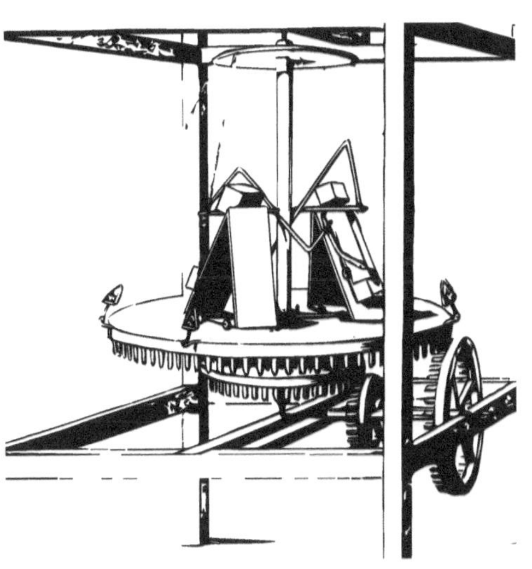

SPUYTEN DUYVIL
New York City

Sincere appreciation to The Danish Arts Foundation for their financial support towards the translation of this book.

THE DANISH ARTS FOUNDATION

Library of Congress Cataloging-in-Publication Data

Names: Himmelstrup, Kristian, 1971- author. | Sokol, Nina, translator.
Title: Tiny shifts / Kristian Himmelstrup ; translated from the Danish by
  Nina Sokol.
Description: New York City : Spuyten Duyvil, 2020.
Identifiers: LCCN 2020010748 | ISBN 9781952419010 (trade paperback)
Subjects: LCSH: Himmelstrup, Kristian, 1971---Translations into English.
Classification: LCC PT8177.18.I48 A2 2020 | DDC 839.813/8--dc23
LC record available at https://lccn.loc.gov/2020010748

The Coin

Come closer, my friend, don't just stand there. Come and make a guess, win a fortune or lose yourself. Keep an eye on the coin, that was what I was going to say, do you see it? It's right here, between my thumb and my index finger. No, that wasn't so tricky, but watch now as I place it under the middle cup, make sure to keep a close eye because I will now begin shuffling the cups ever so slowly. Look, here it is; are you with me? No, don't look at me, look at the coin, the C-O-I-N, I know that it's just a game, that these are nothing but letters to you, but try playing along, you can't lose. In a minute we'll see how closely you've been paying attention, if you have you might just win the jackpot. It's back in the same position as before now, in the middle, I promise I'm not cheating, this time I'll do it a little faster, and I want you to guess: right, middle or left? It's easy, Look, there's a squirrel running across the road! No, just teasing. Now keep an eye on the cups so that you don't get cheated and lose all your money. Okay, I'll stop now. What do you think? The one on the right? Really? Are you certain?

And what if we were to now replace the coins with people? A Turk, a Romanian and a Russian? I know, it can be hard to distinguish between the three, but take a good look at them. They are all equally bad, you're right about that, but only one of them did it: Cut up a girl into pieces with poultry shears, put her remains in a garbage bag and tossed her in a ditch. And keep an eye on them again, because this time I'll hide them under an alibi, send one of them on a business trip to Hanoi, the other down to the grocery store, the third one on a fishing trip with his childhood friend, look, here he is, but keep your eye on the others, too, because one of them has done it, and in a moment I want you to tell me who it is. Of course, they all three have a motive of some kind, that goes without saying, something related to trafficking, money, sex, it doesn't much matter, it's all been seen before and is purely cliché; are you with me? The Turk is on the plane, the Romanian on a fishing trip, the Russian at the grocer's, and I'm starting to shuffle them ever so slowly now, the Russian is on a fishing trip. the Romanian at the grocer's, the girl-- no, the girl is dead, of course; are you even listening? She's still in the garbage bag, lying in the ditch, we have to find out who did it, I'll shuffle one last time and then I'll reveal the alibi. Are you ready? The Russian, the Turk or the editor?

The Editor

It has to do with morals, a sense of decency and proper behavioral patterns, about mankind as being a polypoid organism that starts its journey at the bottom of the sea by being constricted and is transported into the ocean like an empty sack with its toxic threads floating behind it. We are nothing but amoebas, that was what I wanted to say, chemical processes collected in a sack of flesh unreflectively responding to our surroundings. What makes a relief worker expect to get special treatment, for example, or a father kill his daughter with an iron girder, or a woman murder her husband?

My editor sighs and shakes his head as though he doesn't know what to do with me. He has made several unsuccessful attempts now at interrupting me, at breaking into my torrent of speech in order to shift my focus away from thoughts of decency and direct them toward marketability, audience expectation and perceiving books as commercial products in competition with other commercial products.

"You must take its marketability into account," he says once again.

He knows he's being provocative, you can tell by the way he says those words, that's the whole idea, his little crusade against unnecessary narrowness. There is an exaggerated sense of conviction in his tone of voice but the naturalness he aspires to betrays him. Time has truly marched on, it is no longer sufficient to let the temperature in a relationship rise and then park a man's passion in a greenhouse.

Short stories don't sell, and I am well on my way to shooting myself in the foot with this meta story, it bodes well. I can already see him slamming his poor forehead on the table: "Why didn't you write an erotic crime novel, a self-help book, a handbook, a cookbook, a conversation book? No one wants to read about things that don't happen in real life or things they can't translate into useful products that they can utilize in their precious spare time: bread with nettle, a cultivated garden. easy children, a better life. People are stupid, he says, possibly indirectly, but I think that's what I hear him say: people are stupid, they have lost their ability to think in abstract terms, Jussi Adler-Olsen has killed it, brutally, with an awl and a pair of pincers, that sort of thing, first by cutting off the breast nipples with a pair of nail scissors, making the blood stream down the chest, throat, chin, face, so that the blood sputtered and the eyes were forced to close, (he had first hung it up on its head on a meat hook in an abandoned slaughter-house in the Meat District of Copenhagen).

Afterward Jussi can be seen in the spotlight with his hair blown back and an intriguing look in his eye (there must be a fan that has been placed just outside of the periphery of vision). He is wearing a blood-stained apron and he is holding a meat-hook in one hand and a dripping axe in the other. Behind him hangs the ability to think in abstract terms, next to reflection and the desire to read short story collections.

My editor looks up with interest.

He is a little man, the editor, little and bald, his gaze is empty, drained from having to participate in something he can't quite grasp, from trying without succeeding, from wanting too much, transparent blue, with a darker core of recessive ambition. Perhaps it is the light coming from the small windows above him and that falls across his chubby figure, hitting the screen in front of him so that he can barely decipher the text. He extends his hand and readjusts the Venetian blinds.

He has never taken any interest in sports, something which he defiantly proclaims at all the engagements he attends where he entertains the other guests as had he participated in WWII on the German side, and it sounds plausible; his movements are uncoordinated and his stomach bulges out over his belt. On the other hand, he's got power, he feels, verging on the physical. It has on several occasions caused him to get an erection at inopportune moments; on one occasion it was in connection with a female writer making her debut and with whom it was touch and go, and the very thought of rejecting her small, pale pile of papers that lay on the table between them made his prick get hard under the table. He was forced to simulate a telephone conversation and apologetically wave her out the door in order not to get caught. Even though that thought, too, seemed arousing.

"We'll work something out," he said, his hand covering the receiver, and then, in a more enthusiastic tone, "Yes, Morten, hello."

The contents of the books don't interest him all that much, but he enjoys selling them. He focuses on the cover as opposed to the contents, the potential press photos and interviews, as opposed to structure, rhythm and flow. He prefers watching American TV series, drinking coffee down at the square, shelling shrimps on a bathing jetty somewhere in Odsherred. Every so often he enjoys reading, I don't mean to make him sound worse than he is, quick thrillers, preferably beside a pool with an umbrella drink and his feet raised up.

He knows that he shouldn't drink too much, especially when mingling with the crowd within the industry but after a glass he forgets why. He doesn't recall until the following day, and then only vaguely. when brief flashes from the previous evening flutter persistently behind his fervent eyelids; the woman in the red dress who may possibly not have been quite as interested as she seemed to be during the evening, the puzzling glances, the hand signals she gave to her friends, the silent "save me" that her lips seemed to exude, He had originally only intended to be at the party for a few hours, the Busy Editor, to later dutifully retreat, take the bus to Kolding and then the train, but then the girl radiated "take me" so persuasively that he asked the host to reserve a hotel room. He completely forgot the reason why he was there in the first place, it had had something to do with representing the publisher, with showing that the writer is appreciated or, rather, his prick suddenly remembered why it was there and his reptile brain gave into it.

"The red dress, wasn't that why?"

"Yes, that was exactly why, Prick!"

If anyone had the audacity to stand next to the red dress he would interrupt the conversation in order to come between them, if she was going out for a smoke he was too, even though he had quit smoking long ago. But he bummed a cigarette off one of his authors and smoked with great self-confidence out on the terrace under the southern Jutlandic moon which he tried to use as an opening to a pick-up line that didn't work. The red dress smiled, put out her cigarette in a flower pot and went back to the party with him at her heels.

*

He is good at forgiving himself; that's one of his fortes. He can repress the images that haunted his mind the following day and he rummages through his pockets to find the telephone number he never got so that his wife won't find it first. You can never be too careful.

And already the following day he walks through the hallways at the publishing house, creating a positive atmosphere, indefatigably, laughing out loud with his colleagues, flirting intensely with the intern and the PR-girl so that they won't think that he is above talking to them. He brings the publishing house together, his persona unites them in toward a single common goal: him.

He has read several books on modern, appreciative, situational-based leadership, several chapters, at least, as well as the blurb on the backside cover.

He has just come out with a crime novel that has sold a hundred million worldwide and an erotic thriller that has been number 1 on the New York Time's best seller list for the past 38 weeks. It is a rather daring way to run a publishing house in his opinion and both titles are also selling surprisingly well in Denmark and earning millions for the publisher. He smiles as he tells it. They'll quickly be squandered on crappy narrow literature, yet still he feels that he has secured the publishing house and he senses the acknowledgement he gets from the others when he arrives too late to the meeting or chitchats with the employees, like now, as I make my way up in the building in an old, finely paneled elevator. He teasingly places his hand on the intern's screen as I wait for the doors to slide open, adjusts the desk lamp so that it shines right in her eyes, laughs out loud, so that the sound of his laughter resounds through the hallway. I step on the soft carpeting of the publishing house and immediately see the back of him, hear the residuals of his laughter and walk over and position myself behind him.

He doesn't register anything. the only thing that exists in the world right now to him is a female intern who is in on some fun.

I carefully clear my throat.

"Hi Kristian!" he says jovially as he turns, quickly replacing his sultry smile with one that is more professional, one that would make a Formula 1 driver's mechanic envious, faster than they'd be able to loosen a bolt and with approximately the same technical precision. He says something or other publisher-like to the intern and then flings his arm out toward his office.

I am wearing my best clothes, a loose fitting, matching sports jacket and pants, the sleeves of the jacket are slightly too long, something I didn't notice until I saw my reflection in the elevator mirror on the way up and it annoys me now. I need the self-confidence that a proper suit of clothes can give me and this feels completely wrong. Last time I had it on it suited the style of the times but now it's all petered out into legs that are too long and sleeves that are too short.

"Would you like a cup of coffee?" he asks outside the door.

*

"The collection of short stories isn't selling worth a damn. Can't you change it to a novel? I think you can, just erase the titles and replace them with some transitional passages, it shouldn't take you very long."

We are sitting across from one another in light purple designer chairs at the conference table. He drums his fingers slightly on the manuscript lying before him, leans back in his chair and looks over at me.

"That doesn't quite correspond to my original thoughts with the book ."

"No, but you probably shouldn't have too many thoughts about it to begin with. Not if you want to make any sales, which you do." He laughs to himself. I take a sip of coffee. Who doesn't want to make sales?

"Can't someone die at least?" he then asks, and I think, Yes, someone possibly could.

I observe his heavy frame as he talks, the round, slightly glistening head, the sweat on his forehead. A pig, a well-fed pink pig, I think. It's something to do with best-sellers again, ploughing the same furrow in the same vein. Apparently, I should incorporate something with snow and Scandinavian darkness, as well as blonde women, bicycles and a brutal murder, perhaps, misogyny, he brightens up at the thought of his own idea, give the feminists something to get worked up over.

"Why not write something people want to read?" I register him saying, but the words fade into the tapestry, the pictures of popular authors, of a smiling editor next to E.I. James at a reception in London.

His breasts quiver as he speaks. And I catch myself staring at them, at him, his glistening face and I sense that he senses it and finds it unpleasant, but that doesn't stop me, I can be rather persistent. Furthermore, I feel dizzy, as though I'm about to fall over backward through the chair, the carpet, the floor, the building, in slow motion and his trembling breasts are the only things that can prevent it. He talks about front covers he is fond of, with somewhat less self-confidence now, nothing about the content. He turns his chair to search in the white bookshelf, pulls out a pink book, there is the face of a lovely girl and an easy title depicted in gold and black.

I remove my tie and smile at him, ambiguously, I feel: "He removed his tie and smiled ambiguously at him." Diabolically, did he smile diabolically? Forewarningly?

"Here it is," he says and somehow I register this as my cue and do as is expected, hurl myself across the table so that the coffee crashes to the floor and the table tips him out of the designer chair.

He tries crawling away across the carpet, but that's impossible. Nothing happens and I'm on the verge of laughing over the hopelessness of crawling across a carpet instead of trying to solve the problem or turn against the attacker. That's what you get for preferring genre fiction, I think, as I wrap my tie around his neck. I tighten it and hear him rattle, push down on his back with all my might and weigh in, but at that very same moment the PR-girl knocks on the door, opens it ajar and screams when she sees me sitting on top of the editor's back strangling him with a wide-striped tie. I quickly look around, throw myself against the door so that it slams in her face. It was the only solution I could think of. Perhaps I should have initiated a sex scene with her there on the floor at this point in this whole unfortunate affair, right on top of the chubby editor's lifeless corpse?

"Ouch, damn it!"she cries out in the hallway as I jam a chair beneath the door handle, and before I'm done doing that I've already forgotten her. That was about as big an impression she made on me.

Where was I? There was something involving a wide tie and a strangled editor, one of his arms is twitching a little, but there are sounds coming from behind the door once again, my name is being called, urgent and pedagogical, something about being sensible, about not making things worse than they are, and I crawl up on the writing desk, push the window open and squeeze myself out, leave the voices behind me, roll once across the slanting surface before getting to my feet and taking a look around. I am standing on the roof of a four-story building in my slightly oversized suit which I pull tightly around me before disappearing out of the story. I can hear the sound of rhythmic thrusts behind me, someone is trying to break in through the door using their narrow shoulders. They must have given up talking sense to me.

The Chair

He breaks the ice with a hammer, his eyes filled with tears, making rhythmic thrusts so that the cubes smash to tiny fragments inside the bag. He has placed a breadboard underneath it, that much he remembered to do. He dries his eyes in a dishwashing cloth hanging from a hook by the refrigerator before cleaning up the table, rinses a few knives, the breadboard, the steak hammer. He becomes lost in his thoughts by the sink, lets the hot water run as he scrubs with the sponge, round and round, so that the muscles moving under his shirt become visible, the veins on his neck protrude.

Then the doorbell rings.

He collects some packaging, some onion peels, the bloody bag from a roast, and throws it into a black bag standing open on the kitchen floor. He ties it with a knot and drags it through the kitchen and out to the hallway, opens a door to the garage. With some difficulty, he throws the bag out there, shuts the door, checks his clothes in the mirror on his way back, gives a forced smile to his own reflection. He looks tired. In the eating area the table is decorated with flowers and bottle-green candlelights, neatly folded napkins, newly polished silverware which he otherwise never uses, which he doesn't like at all.

He goes out and opens the door.

"I didn't think anyone was home," Hans says, "Iben thought we had mistaken the dates but I was fairly certain that it was tonight." Iben utters a silly laugh. She is fifteen years younger with blond, well-groomed hair and a black leather bag that looks expensive. Behind them he can see their red Volvo below the street light.

"I was just taking out the garbage," he says, looking at his watch. "I didn't realize it had gotten so late."

"Well, we're also five minutes early, I said so to Hans."

"May we come in anyway?" Hans asks.

"No!" he quickly says. but then he checks himself, laughs at his own reaction as though it were a joke. "Of course," he says as he steps to the side. He casts a glance at the garage door, checking to see whether he remembered to shut it behind him. A car parks behind the Volvo, a silver-gray Mercedes station wagon and a middle-aged man gets out, comes round to the other side of the car and opens the door to a leg in net stockings and stilettos that stretches out through the door and then to the figure of a woman in a short dress staggering onto the sidewalk. She waves up at them.

*

He has prepared 16 gin and tonics with crushed ice and lemon slices. The last glass remains left on the tray, untouched. Demonstratively alone. Hans looks around.

"Where is Helle?" he asks.

"She went out to get a chair, but she hasn't come back," he says. "I saw her from the window and she had changed into her long boots and was carrying her purse. She didn't say anything so I actually don't know whether she'll be coming back tonight."

"Oh?"

"We had a fight, nothing major, but she lost her temper and the next thing I heard was the door slam."

Yonna looks over at him with alarm.

"Did she say anything? I mean, about where she was going?"

"Not a word," he says as he smiles somewhat tensely. "Cheers! Let's not let her ruin a perfectly cozy evening for the rest of us!"

"Hear, hear!" several of the others say.

He fetches the bottle of gin and pours himself a refill. "It got a little weak," he apologizes as he empties his glass. He stands for a moment looking at the others, then he clears his throat, "I'd better check on the roast. Please help yourselves."

"Don't you worry about that," William says, laughing, he is already on his way over to the green bottle. He fills the glass halfway with gin and tops it off with tonic.

He stands leaning against the kitchen counter when Yonna enters. He hears the others laughing behind her, someone must have said something funny. The clinking of bottles.

"Do you need help with anything?" she asks. "Now that Helle isn't here you may need a hand with something?"

He casts a glance into the living room where they are busy dispersing themselves into their habitual constellations. Some have seated themselves in the setting with the corner sofa and the Barcelona chairs right across from it.

"Would you mind bringing out some chips for them?" Hans says and then, his voice cracking, "I didn't get a chance to."

"Are you okay?" she asks as she reaches for his hand. He pulls it back.

"Of course I'm okay. Just take the goddamn chips in."

She finds a basket in the closet next to the stove, pours the chips into it and walks into the living room. The sound of her heels against the floor make a cold shiver run down his spine. He stirs the pot once but then turns his back to it and crosses his arms.

"She found the receipt," he says when she returns, in a low but cold voice.

"What receipt?"

"The one from the hotel, of course, what do you think?"

"How should I have known that? Couldn't you have thought of something?"

"I tried, but she knew right away. She's known all along."

"Why did you keep the receipt at all? That wasn't too smart."

"It was in my wallet, I'd forgotten all about it. She wanted to see whether I had a bus ticket she could borrow."

"She can't just go through your things like that."

"I think she's understood that now."

"If Hans ever did that, well, I just don't know what I'd do."

"I could never dream of doing it either, dear," Hans says quietly. He is standing, holding the bowl of chips in front of him and there is no way of knowing how long he's been standing there, but they look at each other. Iben lifts her arms and lets them fall back down to her sides. They can hear the others' voices from the living room, something about a bicycle trip to Jerusalem and someone laughs.

To Jerusalem

He woke up early one morning, changed. He got up, made coffee, fetched the newspaper from the hallway as he always did, read it by the table in the living room; accidents, catastrophes, corrupt politicians and the stage set for war in various places in the world, a plane that had crashed in a jungle in South America. He was the one who had changed, I haven't claimed anything else, the world looked like it always had.

At seven o'clock he sat down on a chair next to his bed and observed his slumbering girlfriend, and that's how he was sitting a half hour later when she woke up. She didn't seem surprised when she opened her eyes and saw him sitting there, but she sensed that he had changed. That observation is now reconfirmed by someone who knows him well, his girlfriend, possibly the one who knows him best. He no longer had any contact with his parents.

He had had a revelation, he said.

"A revelation?" She thought that sounded a bit high-flown but there was no indication of irony in his voice. Therein lay the change, she thought. He had a glow of clarity about him which he hadn't had before, perhaps mixed with a little sense of overbearance as he explained what now seemed in his world to be obvious. Earlier he would tend to ramble and be insecure, very much aware of his own limitations. When there were guests he would often sit smiling quietly after he had finished serving the food. He took every opportunity he could to fetch something out in the kitchen, salt, butter, water, and was the first one to react if someone had managed to spill something.

He had gotten drunk a few times, and that was when one got a little glimpse of what it was Marie had fallen for. He talked about himself, his childhood, a trip to Italy, even about a former girlfriend. The next morning he remained lying in bed for a long time, his stomach churning with shame, swarming about on the verge of nausea.

"Jesus appeared before me, here at the doorway. He said I have to bicycle to Jerusalem."

"Was it an order, or did he just say it?" she asked. She had studied religion for a semester before switching to International Business and Marketing at Copenhagen Business School. She knew that the choice of words wasn't insignificant.

"I mean it, Marie," he said, still with his convinced tone of voice. "I am going to bicycle to Jerusalem."

She wasn't so sure about the part with the bicycle, but he was. She believed that an explanatory statement should have been provided as well and there hadn't been any. He was to bicycle to Jerusalem, end of story.He assumed that the rest would be self-explanatory.

"There will probably be time for more revelations along the way," she believed. "Did he say anything about when you are to leave?"

He didn't answer, turned his back and went out to the kitchen with his coffee cup. "I know it can be hard to accept," he said on his way out of the room.

*

He hadn't pumped his bike tires and ventured forth immediately, she noted, so he wasn't in that much of a rush, apparently. She couldn't exclude the possibility that he had pumped them, of course, but then it would have been in order to take the bike down to the local bike dealer to look at touring bikes and equipment. It had been a long while since he had biked for more than five kilometers, so perhaps it was also just to give it a try. He had grown indolent after having stopped at the university: girlfriend, good food, money, he had of late thought that he ought to get back into shape. In that sense the revelation had come at a very convenient time.

He began preparing for the trip, bought an expensive bicycle, a map, which he studied thoroughly, bicycle wear, energy bars, a nice tool holder in leather. He quit his job, left his beard alone, invited Marie out for a nice dinner, everything he felt one ought to do before embarking on a pilgrimage. He even felt the calling to study the Bible and ignored Marie's skepticism which stood between them like a block. She couldn't help commenting on the price of the bike, the aesthetic qualities of the tools. "Did he order it to be Campagnolo?"

*

One Thursday in May he finally set off. He waved to the few friends that had come out that day, in addition to his cousin Jens and Marie, rode down Strandgade and turned right at Torvegade toward town and further south. He hadn't wanted a big ceremony, it was best to save that for after the task had been accomplished. Marie had nodded.

As he rode in high spirits through town, Marie went up into the apartment and as he made his way to Gammel Køge Road she wandered about somewhat restlessly from room to room, went out to the kitchen and put up some water for coffee, and as he got into a kind of rhythm, nodding to another bicyclist and looked out across the water of Køge Bay, she went out to the balcony to sit down with a cup of coffee and a newspaper in an attempt to suppress it all. They had made an agreement that they were still in a relationship, that they would wait for one another, and that this was something he had to do. It went without saying, he felt, a revelation was not something up for debate; one's free will had to be momentarily suspended when one has received orders from Jesus. "You would have done the same thing," he said, and Marie tried envisioning that Jesus had woken her and not him, that he had stood there in the doorway in his tunic and commanded her to bicycle to the Holy Land, but the image fell apart before she heard herself provide an answer.

Well, anyway, he was biking down through Europe on his new bicycle, occasionally accompanied by others who were on trips of a less ostentatious nature, but aside from that he enjoyed his lonely trek, to feel the road beneath him, the wind against his face, the rhythmic beating of his heart under his jersey. He spoke with children who immediately detected something adventurous as he leaned his densely-packed bicycle against a stand in the small towns in order to forage for the next lap. He slept in fields, behind trees and bales of straw, in sheds and schoolyards and sometimes with hospitable Germans who he happened to meet as he put up his one-man tent. Then he would usually get dinner, regional dishes with potatoes and cabbage and meat, and in return he would tell about his revelation and his endeavour in his elementary school German. He saw them trying to determine whether he was mad or chosen and saw that the conclusion varied depending on whom he visited. Naturally, a family of Hutterites he visited in Blanik nodded acknowledgingly when he told his story, and he remained on their collective bread farm for a week, helping them in the fields and had intense conversations with their leader, an older man dressed in colorless wool who also was in charge of the spiritual development of the children and taught them to praise God both on the guitar and flute as the grown-ups clapped their hands in time.

He had plenty of time to ponder over his own belief, his own significance in the world, and he sensed how he grew into his role as the chosen one for every meter he left behind him. The words "I am one of the chosen," echoed in his mind in time with the guitar strings. At first he had thought a lot about why he had been particularly chosen and what he ought to use his status for and what he could contribute, but after a while he stopped thinking so much about it: He *was*. The doubts, the sense of meaninglessness and insecurity lay like dust on his tracks spread like a thin layer across the highways of northern Jutland. Perhaps that was all he needed to reach, perhaps that had been the goal. At Dresden he ran over a butterfly whose flapping wings could have initiated a tornado somewhere else in the world, he saw it as it lay on the road before him, opening and closing its big, cyan blue wings, a sight whose beauty must have mesmerized him to such a degree that he forgot to yield, but there also had to be a reason why it hadn't flown away, he thought. Yet still he had been perplexed, it was as though the collision was trying to tell him something; that beauty is fleeting, that nature had to yield to instinct, that the human urge for action comes with a price.

Those aren't my banal observations, let me quickly add. They can be read in his diary which he wrote in every evening beneath the glow of the camping lights with a zealous enthusiasm for details; everything had to be documented, he knew that: Aside from thoughts on his faith, on being chosen, and life in general, he wrote a great deal about Marie as well. At first he was ambivalent with regard to his feelings for her, but after a while as his faith grew stronger his love for her consolidated as well; funnily enough, she was necessary in a way for the mission, he wrote, in order to throw his former life into relief, in order to have someone to miss, in order to set his carnal love up against that which was metaphysical, for the loss, in order to really feel the weight of his decision. It doesn't entirely make sense, but you can't really expect that from a diary in which spontaneity and sense impressions are mostly what dominate it and reflections haven't had a chance to properly settle in yet.

*

Back home Marie, of course, managed to find a new boyfriend. It hadn't actually been her intention, but she didn't exactly resist the opportunity when it arose either. At first she had applied herself at her work at the Ministry, seen more of her family and friends, gotten some exercise, and taken care of her skin and health to such an extent that at the end she looked irresistible. She didn't give much thought to her bicycling boyfriend, only when she received one of his rare. soul-searching postcards sent from various cities in Europe as he moved continually south, Brno, Budapest, Resita. He was in the midst of biking his way out of her heart, she thought, to be in line with the tone of his postcards. And ironically enough, his desertion had left a cool air of unapproachability about her which made her, if possible, even more attractive.

Shortly after the postcard from Resita had been dropped down on the hallway floor in Strandgade she met Jorge who worked in the Danish Veterinary and Food Administration, and I have no idea why those two particular people were at the same meeting, their areas of work are, to put it mildly, unrelated, but he invited her out for a drink in the center of town, and her flawless skin, her well-trimmed body and shiny hair, her ironic comments on everything, including about her bicycling, chosen boyfriend, swept him off his feet. He, on the other hand, was exotic, handsome and uncomplicated, all the things her old boyfriend hadn't been. But, first and foremost, he was there right in front of her.

They fell in love, went out for a couple of weeks and gradually started moving in together. When she was offered a foreign posting in Bolivia it was only natural that she asked him whether he would come with her. He would, of course he would, and a few months later they were flying aloft the Atlantic, full of excitement. They drank Campari as they held each other's hands and talked about the new challenges ahead of them. In Spanish. She had been given an intense course by the Ministry and he had helped her. They had practiced in the cool autumn air on her balcony at home while drinking South American wine and looking dreamily across the rooftops of the city. They had stayed up until the early hours of the morning planning everything they wanted to see and do while they were there. And they had also looked forward to it individually, at their separate jobs, looked forward to seeing each other again in the afternoons, longed to talk with each other about their new life after writhing themselves out of the constricting normalities of Denmark.

They rented out their apartment on Christianshavn to a friend who unfortunately perished during a fire when the neighbor in the flat below forgot to turn off the stove from under a pan containing jaggery while he was out buying lemongrass at the local greengrocer. They saw it as a sign, so when the insurance claim was finalized they put it up for sale.

*

Marie and Jorge worked for several years in La Paz but settled down afterward in Tupiza, a beautiful village in southern Bolivia where his parents lived. They started their own company where they worked as guides when Danish friends or tourists came to see the area, and after a few years they bought an abandoned farm which they transformed into a Bed and Breakfast. They also cultivated wine. And in general became a natural part of the village life, especially after they had three children who attended the town's only school. They were all three good children, but the oldest one distinguished himself early, got into Highlands International School in La Paz, studied medicine in the US and later epigenetics, and after several years of applied research his research team managed to develop the first efficient vaccine against cancer.

Perhaps Marie ran into her old boyfriend when she was on vacation in Copenhagen, perhaps they didn't become friends again until Facebook was invented. But when he came home after four weeks of being a tourist in Jerusalem, he knew absolutely nothing about what had happened during the weeks he had made his way down south. He probably wondered why he never received any responses to his postcards since he meticulously indicated the next post office he would reach, but he felt convinced that Marie missed him back home and so he wasn't prepared for the sight of a burnt down apartment and receiving the news about his newly married girlfriend who had left town.

He moved into a small two-room apartment above mine. I seldom heard him, but sometimes he would have guests over who smoked spiced tobacco and sometimes he would play Asian music a little too loudly. It was on a workday in the courtyard that he told about his trip to Israel, the burnt down apartment, his old girlfriend, but it wasn't until he asked me to water his plants while he was away on a trip that I learned the rest of the story through his diary that lay in a drawer in his writing desk under some insurance papers.

The Wind

The same wind that was now blowing him in the face had made Marie's skirt sway earlier that day, a thought which he found pleasant, it had caressed her bosom and tickled her bare legs and now it was making his member feel heavier. Still, he didn't consider it his enemy but perceived it as a greeting from home, in that way they were always in contact with one another even though there were thousands of kilometers between them, he even thought he could hear her whispers in the wind, breathing longingly in his ears like now or angry like yesterday where she had practically shouted at him; every now and then it also carried with it memories of her; her perfume, the smell of her sweaty body under the blankets or her breath in the morning when she turned on her side to give him a kiss.

"You can never see the wind," he hummed but he saw it, of course he did, filled with her colors and scent and mood and in the evening he would cuddle up to it when he was lying in a field in Germany waiting to fall asleep. The same wind had lulled her to sleep, he thought, had been in her lungs and he saw it disappear among the trees which softly rustled as it separated their dark green leaves as it passed through them so that it could reach others that needed it more than he did, back toward Denmark where it would whisper between the reeds at Gurre Lake, breathe a bosomy woman in her ear, blow off the hat of a senile woman in the garden of a nursing home in Amager, gently rock the body of a hanged woman; it would carry all

of this with it, continuing to Thailand where it would dry
the tears off from the cheeks of an older British aristocrat
and make him drive home to fetch his surfboard.

He places his hand over his front teeth when he speaks, consistently, covering his entire mouth with his long, thin fingers, "I got back yesterday," he says through his fingers," and haven't slept the whole night.".

"I almost couldn't recognize you with that complexion, you practically look like a Brit," Martin mutters.

"It's good to see you," says Michael and the rest of us nod in agreement.

"I just had to get down to you. And to Sarah," he says, getting to his feet to give the waitress a hug. Philiip!" she squeals, "It's so goood to seee you!"

"I can sleep when I get old," he continues as he sits down somewhat awkwardly, covering his mouth with one hand and with the other warding off any possible impact with the wooden chair. He moves his telephone and his notebook over to an empty chair so that Sarah can place his breakfast in front of him. She gives his shoulder a little squeeze when she walks back, her hips swaying as she sends him a little smile over her shoulder.

"You old charmer!" says Michael.

"Do you think she might?" Martin asks, his eyes still on Sarah's back.

"I have absolutely no idea what you're referring to," says Philip, "The only thing on my mind is whether the waves will be good for surfing today. I'd rather ride the waves than a young girl," he adds, a smile just barely discernible behind his hand.

"What about Kim?" asks Martin.

"Kim is a different story."

"How are things with her?"

"I have no idea, I just send her the money." "

"Yeah right, you dirty old man."

"It's an act of charity," he says, taking mock offense," there are absolutely no ulterior motives."

Philip breaks off a piece of bread, making the crust crack and crumble on the table. He dips a piece in the soup, pricks a hole in the raw egg yolk and puts it in his mouth. He leans back in his chair, looks across the water that lies smooth as a mirror just below the deck of the restaurant.

"I've missed this," he says quietly and you can sense that he really means it, that the words derive from a place deep within or deep down or wherever the genuine is to be found. It's quite touching, the disintegrating Brit and the sea.

"How was England?" I ask.

"England is England," he says, "if it hadn't been for my father dying, I wouldn't have gone back. But it was all right. I managed to get everything done that I needed to and it wasn't half as bad as I had feared. I even saw my family at the funeral."

"How did that go?"

"Splendidly. My sister had already looted the place, so all the cleaning up and sorting out was left to me. She couldn't bear to throw anything out, she said, but apparently she had no problem taking some of the things down to the auctioneers." He removes his hand from his mouth and runs his fingers through his sparse hair pulling it over the liver spots so that it almost covers the bare spot at the crown of his head. "I couldn't get into contact with my mother, she ordered us around and arranged the entire funeral without displaying the slightest bit of sorrow. It was as though my father had never lived."

"People react to that sort of thing in different ways," Michael says, lifting a spoonful of noodles and ginger up to his mouth. "Couldn't it just be her way of working through her pain?"

Philip doesn't hear him. He waves a fly away with his hand and looks out across the sea. Martin gives us a despondent look, the cheerfulness of the morning has vanished and that doesn't suit him. He picks at his papaya with his fork and can't decide whether or not he should say out loud what it resembles. I can tell that he checks himself.

"I collected all my father's clothes and placed them in bags," Philip says semi-dreamily, his gaze still directed out toward the sea. He even forgets to place his hand back over his mouth and I can see his yellow stained teeth and exposed tooth necks even though I'm sitting next to him. "I carried the sacks out to the car and drove them to the recycling center in town and it's strange because there is an image that has engraved itself in my memory. And it's not the image of my father's corpse or the filled church or the image of all the flowers on his grave which I would have expected it to be, but the image of my father's shoes. They fell out of one of the sacks that I was struggling to get up into the container, a fine pair of brown leather shoes. It was wet and rainy, British weather at its worst, and suddenly there they were, just lying there, my father's brown shoes that didn't contain him, on a shiny wet pavement in Davenport."

And I see him before me standing in the rain holding a black sack, struggling to hold back his tears, the aristocrat who returned home. He hadn't seen his father for twenty years and you sense that there was more to that relationship than he'd like to admit. That he might be in Thailand for other reasons than just to surf.

"They were hardly worn. And it was clear that they had been expensive, and so I was just about to take them, but I'd never use them."

"Wearing out your shoes is a must!" Martin says, laughing. He tips his sunglasses down from his forehead. "I'm going to have to leave. I'm sorry to hear about your father and everything, but I have a massage appointment." He's been waiting for an opportunity to leave and he waves awkwardly as he turns and walks over to his scooter. We can hear him rev up the engine as he makes his way up the hill toward town.

Philip pulls himself together, returns to the beach, toward the deck, toward the morning which is starting to warm up to become yet another warm and humid day autumn day. He fans himself with the menu and covers his mouth with his hand. "It's getting windy after all," he says as he smiles.

Autumn

Last night I finally dreamed about my husband. He came toward me, smiling and whole and I myself woke up with a smile chiseled onto my tired face. I might just as well cry, I thought.

We sat down on a blanket in the garden and it must have been autumn because yellow leaves were lying on the grass, a rake was leaning against a privet hedge, and the blood-red tops of some trees were reflected in a lake. Perhaps it wasn't a garden at all but a lake that possibly extended as far as the eye could see, now come to think of it, but where had it been, then, in a park or by the sea? A river in Hell, because it seemed the river was rushing, or maybe it's just the dream dissolving, the images that are falling apart, the lake that was emptied. Anyway, the important thing isn't the water, I don't know why I'm losing myself in that particular scene, or rather: I know why. I want so badly to remember it all again, the trees, the scent of wool and autumn, the lake. Perhaps some of that might be important, and as I try to recall it he disappears; if I get hold of a thread, the rest unravels, and as I write this he fades out together with the lake. That which was so real turns into nothing and so I must insist: I dreamed about my husband, finally, the important thing was him, not the lake or the leaves, wearing an Icelandic sweater that smelled like wool. Had it rained? The grass was dry, the leaves, except for the ones that were moving and reflected in the mirror of the lake, the blanket we were sitting on. It was white with distorted blue figures,

"

an elephant, perhaps, a fish, like a neanderthal man would have drawn it in a cave.

My husband opened his mouth, said something which I can't remember or didn't hear and I asked what he said, am asking what he said.

"Nothing," he answers and smiles. He was just as he was, as he should be, and I reach out my hand toward his side of the bed.

"It's all right," he said?

*

I've dreamed about my husband before, I contradict myself, his round, red face, his empty gaze. For long periods of time I couldn't avoid dreaming about my husband, the staring eyes whose emptiness could easily be interpreted as judgmental, usually there was nothing left when I woke up other than his staring eyes.

A glimpse of desperation?

It's six years ago since he died and I have been waiting to be allowed to dream about him, the way he looked when he was himself. Before the cancer managed to suck out all the life from him, first the mass of him, his energy, his intellectual wherewithal, his good mood; it was like a greedy child with a straw that sucked everything up until it left him sitting like a salivating imbecile in a wheelchair, skin and bones in soft clothes. Smiling on command, nodding at my little stories, grunting at my questions.

It's hard to say whether he understood that I would put an end to it before I actually did. I tried to talk with him about it, I told him about it and he nodded at the right places, a brief glimpse of clarity behind all the transparency? I said that I couldn't manage it anymore, alone, but that I couldn't bear the thought of him wearing hospital clothes at a hospice. I sat next to the bed and cried and he stared at me. Give me a sign, I cried, and he lifted his hand, ever so slightly he lifted it from the blanket, trembling.

I went out to the kitchen, poured a big glass of whiskey from the bottle on the table, went back and smothered him with a pillow stuffed with eiderdown. I can still feel the cold cotton cover against my palm, the red stripes. I had been considering it for a long time, whether or not to do it, the method, the sense of guilt, so I didn't think so much about it as I did it, yet still, I wasn't prepared for the desperate look in his eyes as he saw the pillow approaching him, the trembling that went through his body and finally his slack limbs below the blanket.

*

I have done everything I could to remember him as he was. I've looked at vacation pictures and watched videos of us laughing and waving and swimming in the Adriatic, playing with the kids in the yard. Tried to commit to memory the image of his brown face, his muscular torso in the waves, his thoughtful smile out in the yard on an autumn day. But the images of his dying body and the last desperate look he gave me have so far been much stronger.

But last night I had a dream about my husband. He was sitting in our yard wearing the Icelandic sweater i gave him for his 50th birthday. It had just been raining, there was the smell of wool and autumn, the yellow leaves which he had just raked into a pile. He placed the rake against the fence when I brought out the juice. We unfolded a blanket and sat down on the grass.

"I'm sorry," I said and he just smiled back.

"That's okay," he finally said.

GRIFFIN

She sits in the chair and looks out the window, a big window with double glazing and safety latches. A distinct silhouette of a bird has been pasted on the window but the woodwork around the glass has decayed which she doesn't notice until now. It needs to be painted and must have needed it for a long time. She can't remember when she had it painted last.

Time passes, Mogens died.

Time passed and Mogens died, that's how she thinks. It started with the window, now it's suddenly back to Mogens.

It was winter when Mogens died. That must be why she's thinking of him now. Did he paint the window or did she shut it to stop the draught from coming in, to shield him from it? He died anyway and now the windows need to be painted, need nursing, need a little tender loving care.

A lot of things do. She looks around. The grandfather clock emits a rattling sound as though it has to pull itself together to strike but doesn't have the energy for it after all. She looks at the dial with an unfocused gaze but knows that it must be either a quarter to or a quarter past whatever hour it is.

She doesn't really need to know more.

She is just about to get up when a bird lands on the stone circle outside. She starts a little when it lands. It's big and usually only a titmouse or sparrow of some kind would enter her yard, and every now and then magpies or the odd raven.

Oh yes, and blackbirds.

At rare intervals a seagull might show up, and they can be surprisingly big and eerie looking up close with their cold, soulless eyes. This one is both big and different, it's frightening, she squints her eyes, its neck is scrawny and reddish. Long and naked.

A vulture?

It stares at her with its tiny black eyes and she turns her head away toward the kitchen, where the door is standing ajar.

"Ugh," she thinks as she shudders. When she looks back out the window it is gone, flown black to wherever it came from.

She carries the encounter with her into the kitchen, dragging her feet, weighed down by the bird's gaze, pregnant with fate and ill omens. It has chiseled itself into her face as furrows.

Perhaps they had been there already?

She goes out to the hallway and puts on her coat, she doesn't know why, she thought she was going to make a cup of tea. Perhaps she would have liked some cake to go with the tea, she's not sure. Maybe she just needs to go out.

There are no vultures in Denmark, she thinks, this time very clearly. There are sparrows and hawks and buzzards and seagulls but no vultures. She's quite certain of that, she's watched a number of animal programmes on TV. Perhaps some birds of prey belong to the the same family as vultures, in which case it is no doubt a calm and civilized family. She goes down the steps of the house, walks down through the garden path and out onto the sidewalk. She looks around before trodding down the road toward the water.

She instinctively crosses to the other side of the street when she sees a couple of young people walking in her direction. There's a reason why she's managed to get this old. Her left arm jerks a little when she sees that one of them is wearing a scarf. She doesn't turn her head, just registers it through the corner of her eye, a scarf, whereupon her arm jerks from fear. It's not conscious on her part, her arm just does it on its own, responds to a possible threat. One's bodily intelligence is greater than one tends to assume, she thinks.

People can dress however they like, she would say at any given time, defending human rights, things like that. Just not here. A scarf, what does anyone have to run around looking like that for, anyway?

She doesn't know why they do it but she knows it's not a pretty sight and that it doesn't belong here. She has nothing against foreigners but she doesn't care for the things that result from their coming here: rapes, crime, vandalism, gangs. The negroes are the worst ones, that's clear as day.

She likes neatness and light colors.

A cat saunters out further up the street and sits down on the curb. A broad head, short snout, chubby cheeks. Cheeks? Big, round, good-natured eyes. It must be a Persian cat she concludes, its fur is fine and expensive and flutters orange shades in the wind.

But it's not called negro anymore, is it? She doesn't understand why they have to keep changing things all the time. Now when everyone knows what's being referred to, is it really necessary to confuse things?

She hears a scream high above her head, sees a shadow create circles on the sidewalk, pulls her coat tighter around her neck, leans forward and walks slightly faster.

To be honest, she really thinks they should go home. But, of course, you can't say that out loud, you can't even think it. If it were up to the politicians at Christiansborg, you wouldn't be allowed to think it. Of that she's fairly convinced.

Things were so good in the past.

She keeps an eye on the shadow on the sidewalk, the cat on the street, her own brown shoes below the coat. The sound it makes when she walks, the asynchronous beating of her heart, the screams above her head.

When she reaches the cat she stops, lets her arms fall down by her side so that her neck becomes completely exposed. She feels like sitting down and petting the cat. There is something about its eyes, but she also knows that she really shouldn't. One just never knows.

She stands like that for a long time, a small dejected figure. Above her the screams intensify until they finally cease altogether. The creature up there folds its wings and dives, something she can't possibly know, but she feels the hairs on the back of her naked neck stand up and sees the shadow on the street before her grow. It spreads its claws and sinks them into the Persian cat and together they fly off, the cat like a ball of yarn below the strange creature.

A griffin, she thinks, could it be a griffin? She turns around, absorbed in her own thoughts. She no longer feels like cake.

The Cap

Chai Apaporn liked cake, but aside from that he didn't have that many interests. He wasn't particularly tall either. He would wear khaki colored pants, red socks, a light blue shirt, sometimes a cap. He had once had a wife named Vera, but he didn't anymore. What he did have, though, was black hair that was cut very short at the sides mostly because that was the only style his barber could manage. Chai would sit down in his usual black chair at the parlor, the barber would say "short," perhaps followed by a question mark, "short?" Chai would nod and he'd end up looking like this, with bangs and basically no side burns. On a good day he thought he looked like an older version of David Beckham, a little. On a bad day he looked like everybody else in Cambodia.

He had an Aprillo scooter with a picture of Snoopy on the front fender. When he rode through town in the afternoons he would wear a blue mask that covered both his nose and mouth which, reputedly, would stop any dangerous particles from entering his organism and ultimately finishing him off.

He liked noodles with vegetables, but who didn't?

He didn't have a girlfriend, it had been a long time since he had had one but he did have an eye for a slender girl with long hair, small round breasts and the sweetest smile. He sometimes escorted her in the mornings on his way through town. When he caught up with her he would slow down his Aprillo and follow close behind hers, trying to catch her scent (which was spicy sweet, perhaps

she worked in a kitchen), trying to form an impression
of her body through her clothes with the help of one of
her shoulder blades or breasts that stretched the material
of the shirt. She had the most charming, worn out sailor
shirt and whenever she wore it (and he happened to see
it) he would float back home on his scooter in a state of
ecstasy after she turned off at Oknha Chhun. He could
ride without holding onto the handlebars, his arms spread
out to the sides like a bird, down along Mekong, until the
speed of the scooter subsided and he had to gas it up with
his right hand.

During his less euphoric moments he worked as a
security guard for a western software company. He would
sit in a shed just outside the main building with a gun,
which didn't work, wearing a uniform that had stars on at
the shoulders. In the evenings he would swing a mosquito
swatter and with each blow he would hit a handful of
insects that would crackle electrically, lighting up the
darkness around him. He wouldn't feel so alone then, the
air was full of life, and the more he swung the swatter the
more mosquitoes there seemed to be. When his shift was
over he would, in the light of the dawn, see them lying
in small piles all around him. He would usually avoid
looking at them, but he knew they were lying there, dead,
all around his chair, charred, crippled. They were through
flying around with all their diseases, their malaria, brain
infections and tropical fevers. Every night he was doing
the country a service, though possibly a minor one, but
if everyone acted just as responsibly as he did, they could
potentially go far.

He hadn't always been a security guard, to put it
mildly. He had played much bigger roles in the theater of

life, but he didn't make a big display of it. He saw to his work and minded his own business, rode his Aprillo, ate his noodles, swung his swatter, cast sidelong glances at the girl in the sailor shirt.

He avoided social interaction at all costs, in that sense the job as a security guard suited him perfectly. There were times when communicating with individuals in his immediate surroundings couldn't be avoided, in which case he would keep it at a minimum. He would order his noodles at the street kitchen below the apartment, his household staples at the market from the same old woman, always the same one. He smiled as he handed her his crumpled bank notes, mumbling a thank you.

He also had a dog that seemed to go by the name of Wiener. At least that's what it looked like. It was his sole and therefore his best companion. It slept in his bed, lay on his lap when he watched American movies on his DVD in order to improve his English, it barked at the neighbor's children when they played on the staircase.

He could go off on a trance whenever he saw kids playing ball in the park, or adults talking with each other around a hot barbecue. He could catch himself staring at an empty garbage can on the street or a heap of turned over garbage that could, in the hours of dusk, suddenly resemble a pile of human corpses, remnants of cloth, hair, bones.

Aside from that he was doing just fine, he could manage getting his life to hang together.

If someone were to look at him for too long a time, while he observed children, for example, he would remove his sunglasses from his pocket, politely nod to the individual in question and take a detour back home. . And he would take one more look around and down the street, before entering his building.

He couldn't recognize the faces of the ones they let go, you couldn't expect that either. Though there may not have been that many of them but time had passed and they had changed, grown fat, long-haired and old. Some of them had only been children back then, how could he possibly recognize them now, twenty years later? But he knew they were there, of course he did. And he knew that they were keeping an eye on him, would spot him in the crowd. For what? Redress? An erection? To alter what happened? He had never been able to understand it. They let them go and yet they wanted revenge which you'd have to say was somewhat ironic. Wasn't it enough that the deceased were haunting the eyes of the children in the park or of those young people or adults he passed on the sidewalk, reminding him of the one of many he had thrashed to death with a bamboo cane? Their almost offended, imploring gaze as they lay tied down to the iron bed or as he lowered them down from the pole and forced their heads down under the water in the big barrels below until they fainted.

He himself had only been a boy back then even though he looked older than he was. With his thin beard, sinewy arms and callous look in his eyes, his face, in fact, his whole body. He had felt like an adult, he fulfilled his role as an adult. And he had appreciated the responsibility that the older ones had bestowed on him.

*

He actually didn't feel relieved when they came to fetch him on a sunny Tuesday in April. Someone must have finally recognized him. They were waiting for him in front of the staircase to his small apartment and he parked his scooter at the curb and went over and gave them a formal greeting as he extended his hand. He was wearing his khaki-colored pants, red socks and light blue shirt.

The cap had been taken by the wind on his way home, he had lifted it as he somewhat rashly passed the girl in the sailor shirt and when she had smiled at him he had lost it from sheer nervousness.

So close to joy.

CORDUROY EXPLOSIONS

The air is still among the blossoming trees which I am incapable of classifying, little white explosions of velvet against the blue sky. Sweat is already trickling down beneath my shirt, down my legs and the air feels like the embrace of a feverish terminal patient, the same hot breath against one's neck, the glassy eyes, the unnatural and dull heat of a dying body.

I am walking on bones, that's what it feels like. I am walking on bones across the lawn which was once a schoolyard, across the flagstones, inside the school building. I hear what I think is the echo of happy children that have played among the trees, whispered during classes, passed small notes to one another between the desks.

That's where I see her.

Her face is harmonious, serious with fine, straight eyebrows above her pitch dark eyes and in the middle of her face: a cute little snub nose. Her hair goes down to the middle of her cheek, newly combed in a glossy side parting. She is wearing a dark shirt, buttoned all the way up to her neck. Her gaze is intense and there isn't a hint of a smile on her face, though neither is there any spite or downright fear. An expectant uneasiness, rather, as though she doesn't quite know what this is all about but doesn't expect it to be anything good.

The picture was taken in 1977 and she's the type of girl I would have fallen in love with if she had lived in West Jutland. She would have been a few years older than me, exotic and fascinating with her dark hair and intense, black eyes.

I was six years old in 1977. I lived in Vejrup in a former farm house, so far so good, we didn't cultivate the soil but the former owners had. We had a stable and a hayloft which we converted into bedrooms for my brother and me, as well as a guest room and a table tennis room. My mother also tried to start a vegetable garden and some berry bushes, in the summer we would pick blackberries, red currants, and gooseberries, the juice of which we would suck out from under the peel before they were completely ripe and we found wild strawberries wherever they were hiding around the property.

My father wasn't exactly a nature lover but he liked the work that living in nature entailed: weeding, cutting, felling and chopping. Putting on his dirty shorts, his short-sleeved shirt in order to get some work done and chop potential worries away. He would be out working until the sun went down, collecting unwanted nature in small piles which he would later dump into a plaintive wheelbarrow and transport to the compost heap in the backyard.

In the middle of the yard there was a big tree which we would climb or sit below and talk about life and the world and that sort of thing. That is probably where I would have taken the girl with the parted hair and the serious looking eyes, perhaps we could have carved our names in the bark at some point, strung strawberries on stalks of straw or played soccer on the lawn in front of the house? The bark was thick and somehow the tree indicated safety, perhaps it was something unconscious, primordial: roots, nature, history. What did I know?

What do I know?

Not far from the school building where I am now standing there is a beautiful tree against which, in the girl's time, infants would be swung so that their soft skulls would be squashed against its trunk. It had been the soldiers of the agrarian socialist brigade that had held the children by their small feet and swung them against the trunk which received them, motionless and mute, unable to lose its leaves in grief, bleed resin or take revenge in the night tip-toeing on its roots.

They did it to all the infants of their enemies, hit them against the tree which at the end was muddied with blood and brain matter. They did it without concerning themselves with what thoughts the little brains might possibly have had later, what kind of adults they might have been. Sometimes they would subsequently throw the corpses into the air and fire at them like big clay pigeons. Was it for amusement? I imagine them laughing as they did it, that they loaded their rifles and fired at the corpses, all the while laughing. Just like in a movie that wants to show how evil and callous humans can be (beyond anyone's comprehension).

And thus human life is shaped differently, all depending on where you were born. All depending on what sperm cell penetrated through the membrane of which egg and all depending on what man copulated with what woman, you grow up in a privileged home in Jutland climbing trees in your backyard watching your father raking the weeds, travel--or you are picked up by a truck, photographed, tortured and die.

I take a step back and see her face disappear amongst numerous pictures of other faces hanging there, thousands of despairing eyes, children's, adults', old people's. For some reason the most malicious devils in the world have always had a burning desire to document their atrocities, with the zeal of any self-respecting accountant they have kept track of their inhumanity.

*

Shortly after the picture was taken, in a torturous-looking chair equipped with an iron grip to keep her head in place, the girl was led into a small, clumsy cell made of brick on the third floor of the school building. She had been puzzled by the chair, their commandeering voices, their firm grip on her arm, not until now did she understand.

When they had picked her up along with her parents they had painstakingly explained to her that all they wanted was to talk with them and that they couldn't let her stay home alone. When they came to the school they just wanted to take a picture of her. Her mother had screamed when they had been separated in the courtyard but she still hadn't understood any of it. Her mother had whispered in her ear during the entire trip that it was all going to be okay, that it was a mistake, the men wouldn't harm them. But they had hit her mother on the mouth when she screamed and now she herself was sitting with a chain around her leg in a cell where it was practically impossible to sit down. She could hear the sound of moaning and whimpering voices all around her and it was hot, infernally hot, as hot as a thousand summer days, as hot as it had been sitting around the grill table yesterday.

47

She thought about the evening with her family and was just about to forget where she was but then she looked around and remembered. She couldn't see any way out, or any sign of hope. Her mother and father weren't here and even if she were to cry no one would console her, that much she grasped. But she didn't understand why, wasn't it a law of nature that grown-ups should always console crying children?

And things weren't going to improve in the coming months. They asked her questions she didn't understand, threatened her to sign her name on a piece of paper upon which they had written a long story in advance of their own devise. At that point they had already several times tied her to the iron bed where they would make her lie several hours at a time. Once a day she would get boiled water with rice, once a week she would get a bath, a pail of water thrown through the window from the outside on the assembled group of naked children. She would often get hit by a boy with sparse facial hair.

The last day he was alone with her in the room and he would grope her in between blows with the bamboo cane, moaning derogatory words he tightened the screws in her handcuffs. As though it was all her fault. His hardened face was the last thing she saw (she looked for signs of compassion up to the very last) while she was just another corpse he dragged out to the pile to be picked up. Perhaps he lit a cigarette and looked up at the sky where a bird of prey circled the schoolyard and cotton-like clouds quietly floated by in the afternoon heat. Perhaps he was given a pat on the shoulder by one of his older friends who cracked yet another joke about their job.

At any rate, he survived and in a later reality he even got a job working for a western IT firm the building of which he would often sit in front of swinging an insect squatter in the air.

Just like I continue walking, past the rows of pictures and out into the same sun, the same clouds, the same sky. And continue my life as though evilness is a historical phenomenon. As though I weren't of the same species, don't have it in me, a little bit of them in me, the sun shining, the birds singing, the grass growing, an indefinable bird of prey circling the schoolyard.

Stormy Weather

Try to imagine the following: Two children are playing in the living room, you can hear their voices but you can't hear what they're talking about and it is merely an indefinable something in the quality of their voices, in the rhythms of their sentences that make you realize that a conflict between them is under way, a little bit of stormy weather between siblings. They are broadcasting on the channel that insists on a conflict and which disturbingly meddles with your central nervous system, making you put down your newspaper, carefully fold it and get up before the storm breaks out for real, sending their little ships out on a collision course. It is your job to prevent it, your most important job is to ensure that they sail through their childhood in fair weather, shield them from their own and others' demons.

You walk through the kitchen where you take a sip of the cold coffee you forgot to drink and continue out into the hallway and at this point you are able to distinguish words, many of them abusive words like fuck and bitch and idiot uttered quickly one after the other, and when you enter the living room you see that the children have gotten up from their paintings, a small can of paint has toppled over, leaving an image of a green hot air balloon across the floor, or a treetop, rather, a paintbrush on the floor is its trunk, a short string could be the snake that escaped. One of the children pulls back her arm to strike a blow, you see the bad temper she is in radiating from her whole being, her face is red, her attitude is one of aggrievement and of revenge incarnate. She is just about to swing her arm, you can practically see the muscles around her shoulder contract when something unexpected happens. She pixelates and you frown and try to focus, but what you saw was true, the children are fluttering before you, are slowly dissolving, pixel by pixel, then faster, are reassembled in new ways, as for example now, where they are sitting back down on the floor, have turned the paint can right side up, making the tree flow back in, and they are excitedly painting on one another's drawings, calling each other names but then they get back up again, directly contrary to the chronology, their legs grow, their chests expand and become wider, their bodies gain mass, beards grow on their smooth skins, bushy eyebrows, unruly hair. Wearing animal hides they stand, dizzy, around a sacrificial bonfire, one of them holding a club in his hand, and before you can interfere one of them has managed to smash the skull of the other, summoned God's anger and run away from the group of soldiers that come running in now from the outside, more and more, until they fill the room and a small man in a tight uniform gets up on a podium in front of them, where the writing desk stood just a moment ago, lifts his arm in salute, screaming incomprehensible orders. A row of missiles are positioned in place and ascend under a canon-like thunder; the man disappears but his voice lingers in the air, changes into a buzz that melts into one with the missiles that now ascend amid thunder; you follow them with your eyes shielding them with your hand against the sun until they strike the room. A mushroom cloud grows all at once far away (you can see the entire cloud) and close by (in the room). You feel the pressure against your eyes, people fleeing with remnants of clothes burnt to their skin, a child crying, your daughter who clutched her cheek with a shocked look in her eyes.

52

MILK

She is following us until it becomes unpleasant, pulls at our arm, implores. She practically pushes her infant into our arms, waving its empty bottle.

"I don't want money," she says, "I just want some milk for my child." She points to a supermarket on the other side of the street. Her voice is that of a girl's, a hoarse girl, her body is scrawny, her clothes worn. She has clearly chosen us to save this evening's dinner for the child, she let hundreds of locals pass her without saying a word, but rushed decisively over to us, the incarnation of the injustice of the world, the Fat Whites.

I don't have the energy for it, fling my arms about so she can see how unsuitable it is, how pushy, wrong, how *hard* it is to be confronted with. After all, I didn't ask to be born in Denmark, to get that burden placed on my porcelain white shoulders.

I continue walking without looking back, drag my kids along with me.

"We can't save them all, she'll have to think of a more sustainable way to get the child food," I explain and my daughter nods gravely. She grasps that, with the corner of her budding intellect. "What will happen when she's drunk the milk we've bought for it? She'll just be facing the same problem."

"But at least she'd be full today," my daughter attempts, and I shake my head forbearingly."

The girl follows us and grabs hold of my polo shirt, forcing me to remove her hand and turn around threateningly before she understands and looks around in search of more receptive patrons.

But it relieves us only for a brief period of time, they are also sitting in front of the supermarket, all the city's cripples, and they have exposed their artificial limbs for all to see in a tableau that replicates that of the supermarket in back of them. How large is your sense of compassion, you indulger, what would you give to see my artificial limbs? A cutlet in a cold counter, a free-range pig, an organically raised pig.

And when we are through doling out, to what would you then give the money? To the right hand lying extended on the sidewalk next to the leg with a bolt thread, to the head still attached to the torso, or to the scrawny children next to them, the leper guy, the cripple on the skateboard?

That is how we all sell ourselves the best, I think, it's a study in market economy. It's very informative. We turn our best side to the photographer, display our starving children, our mongoloid deformed little sister, our own blemishes and unsavorinesses. Our Westen bodies in blue Lacoste-polo shirts, our smiles in a tired face.

THE DO-GOODER

He splashes water onto his face, looks at his own reflection in the mirror, at how it runs down his cheeks, collects itself as small beads around his eyebrows, drips down into the sink. He has a pointed nose, hollow cheeks, a distinctly carved face which the moisture has now given a much needed sensual lift. Once he was sailing and in brief flashes he remembers it, the salt water, the wind, the sun, the medals on the bulletin board in his room and he feels a pang of yearning in his side that quickly subsides. It's all so long ago, and now he's standing here, in a suit and with polished shoes, stains of perspiration showing under his arms and a subsiding yearning in his side. That was back when he was a fanatic doing fantastically, he thinks, when he would weigh his food and would become sick if he took a bite from a small cake. Back then he was convinced that it was a sheer physical reaction, now he isn't so sure, now he is able to eat both fast food and chocolate without any problems; and, after the kids have been put to bed, even fruit gum.

Back then he was convinced of so many things.

He wipes his face with a paper towel that comes out of the shiny box hanging next to the sink.

"That was a long visit," says the woman waiting for him outside. She has a small piece of roller luggage in front of her which she rolls over to him, hands him the luggage handle which has been warmed by her impatient hand.

"Sorry." He looks down at his shoes which were expensive. He bought them when they were together in China a few months ago. It had been his first trip and already on the second night she had hinted that it would be a good idea to upgrade his footwear. He would have to take on the role, look like someone who wanted respect. And his footwear would be a good place to start.

He bought the shoes the next morning in an American-inspired shopping center that solely sold western brands. She sent him there during a break between meetings and he found it a bit ridiculous. But he respected her and even possibly understood her and now he was happy that he had bought the shoes.

"Not to rush you or anything, but we're already late. We're meeting a group of NGOs in an hour."

"I know. I was actually the one who arranged it," he mutters.

She looks at him and nods in acknowledgment, according to his interpretation. She isn't the most empathic person in the world, but she respects work and she must be able to see that he is working himself to the bone. He's here to make a difference, which he also feels that he's doing.

"Nice suit," she then says.

*

They pass the line of waiting people, for some reason or other only one passport control booth is open and it smells of sweat and morning breath here. He sees how most people are trying to conceal their irritation and impatience by closing their eyes, humming and jumping up and down a little bit in place. A child is crying, a German utters a few curses against the system from his spot in the back of the line. The fat woman behind the glass window takes her time with each individual, thoroughly examining the passports, studying the owners' face before placing the stamp. It is a bureaucratic ballet, the choreography of which has been thoroughly rehearsed, that's what authority looks like, that's what powerlessness looks like.

"Here," she says as she pushes the passports under the glass with the same reserved smile, a second's worth of feigned friendliness to each applicant.

They show their passports to an inspector at the exit for diplomats and he nods and waves them further on, through the lounge where they will be picked up by their contact person.

"Welcome to Malaysia," she says in flawless English. "My name is Lydia." She walks in front of them toward the exit as she tells them that the weather is pleasant, though it has rained for a few days but that they made sure to have good weather upon their arrival.

He smiles and mutters something in response.

She smells pleasantly of soap and lavender and he can't help looking at her slender calves under her dark blue skirt. He can see her muscles moving underneath her nylon stockings with every step she takes.

She holds the door open for them and they step out into the air that caresses his face, that's how it feels, like slender fingers in silk gloves. She points toward a long Mercedes the doors of which are open, and he steps in.

The limousine drives them to the Intercontinental Hotel where a doorman immediately steps out to take their luggage. He carries it through the lobby, struggling to conceal how overwhelmed he is: the shiny marble floor, the columns, the stairs that practically float up to the second floor, the gigantic crystal chandelier that looks like it has sucked itself onto the ceiling like a lavish ball gown. It resembles a movie and Lydia is the Asian guest star, he himself perhaps the secret agent who ends up saving the world. And screwing the Asian guest star who goes over to the reception desk to sort out their papers and returns with their key cards and some papers.

"We'll assemble in the meeting room on the second floor in twenty minutes," she says. "I thought you'd want a little time to powder your noses first. I'll just check and make sure that everything is in order and then we'll meet there."

They nod. Lydia pushes the button on the elevator and he follows behind the person responsible for their stay in the country.

*

The room is, of course, huge. He would have sworn that that sort of thing meant nothing to him but it's hard not to find it pleasant if you're truly honest with yourself. That wasn't the reason why he applied for the job and he still finds it tasteless but he actually couldn't have chosen anything cheaper even if he wanted to. There are certain standards that must be upheld and it would have been a hopeless fight had he insisted on staying in a tourist hotel.

You have to choose your battles carefully.

"Remember to enjoy it," his wife said when he told her that they were going to fly executive class and showed her pictures of the five-star hotel they would be staying at. "You've deserved it, you've worked to the bone for this mission. Now don't go having any moral scruples."

He had always been idealistic, he still is. He thinks of the flight and the hotel as necessary ornaments, like the shoes, precisely like the shoes. . In earlier times he would have found it reprehensible and irresponsible, resisted it, but he has started to understand the system. It is necessary that one looks presentable when representing the mission, that one is well rested when one arrives there, that one radiates a sense of exuberance.

He checks the minibar, unscrews the cap of a bottle of Bailey's and pours the contents over some ice cubes in a sturdy glass and carries it over to the window where the view sends him into a trance: Downtown Kuala Lumpur. He sits down in the soft sofa and turns on the TV, a Malaysian version of X-factor. He skims through the channels and continues on to the selection of porno movies, but then his boss knocks on the door and he quickly turns it off. .

"On my way!" he shouts as he takes out his leather briefcase, quickly checks its contents and walks over to open the door. The carpet pleasantly gives way for each step he takes, he practically feels like he is floating.

*

They have a drink after the meeting up in the bar with a view of the entire skyline, expensive bottles and an exceptionally nice bartender. Lydia is there, too, wearing a short, black dress.

"The next round's on me," he says. "What'll you have?" He's already gotten up.

"Sit back down," says Patricia. She pauses to give her words time to soak in and, giving him a serious look, says, "They were certainly a couple of very idealistic young people we just met." She hands him the Mission's gold card. "There! This is now officially a professional meeting and it is only reasonable that we get the refreshments covered."

He takes the card hesitantly, casts a quick glance at Lydia who smiles back and then crosses the patterned carpet over to the bar. The meeting had dealt with the western exploitation of the entire region, the miserable conditions in the factories, entire villages that were suffering from toxic spills by industry, deformed children and child labor. They had welcomed the reports from the young NGOs, he had taken down the minutes, Patricia had listened. Every so often she had asked for a little clarification, mostly to exhibit attention and at one point she leaned towards him and explained how she wanted something formulated. She shook hands and promised to have a look at the whole thing when she got home. Everything went according to protocol and it was all very satisfying. And when he gets home he'll make a summary of it in a big report which no one will ever read, he knows that too well. Yet still he can't see any better way to organize the system. What he is doing is necessary.

He's already working through some formulations for the report in his mind, testing various loaded types of expressions on himself as he waits at the bar, mild forms of criticism, harmless reprimands and suggestions to the Laotian civil service.

He orders a gin and tonic and is gibed at for his conservative choice when he brings them down. He hadn't dared to order any of the colorfully-named drinks on the menu because he was afraid that it would demonstrate poor judgment and taste on his part, be too charter-like. But apparently Patricia doesn't seem to have any of those concerns when it's her turn to order, she chooses the most expensive drink on the menu, something that has sugar on the edges of the glass,

"You can't go wrong with this."

Later Lydia follows suit, orders a bottle of Cristal and laughs when Patricia, taking mock offense, asks how many child laborers could have been given an education for that money. She parodies one of the participants of the meeting, who, in his eagerness, had practically spit as he spoke.

The mood has become rather unrestrained, he has got some color in his cheeks and is almost smiling.

*

It grew late before he went to bed. He tried to leave several times but Patricia and Lydia ganged up on him and convinced him to stay. At one point Lydia had taken hold of his hand under the table and he didn't know what to do so he didn't do anything and kept her hand in his. Lydia continued talking with Patricia who gave him a conspiratorial smile. And then he suddenly felt the warmth from her soft palm spread to his after all, up along his underarm to his chest and after yet another glass of champagne, down to the pit of his stomach. Suddenly he saw it all before him: Lydia under him on the couch of his big bedroom with her dark blue skirt pulled up, her silk stockings pulled down, the view of the city, the minibar. But some corner of his rational mind must have taken over because he twisted his hand loose, gently, and excused himself, saying he had to go to the bathroom. From there he went up to bed, he would have to deal with all the teasing tomorrow.

It wasn't until the third day that he gave up the unmatched battle. Lydia had escalated her offense, making it practically unbearable to be him. He felt that he no longer had any choice, any willpower, it had been broken down by all the drinks, by all the time away from his wife, by the random touches and flirtatious glances the past days, and so he couldn't be blamed for what was bound to happen. It seemed like the only sensible, the only *right* thing to do.

*

The limousine drove them to the airport the following day but when they were about to check in the diplomat desk wasn't open so they had to queue up with the other ordinary passengers. Caught in the smell of sweat and hillbilly small talk. He felt his frustration building up as he approached the pale queer standing behind the counter in his light blue uniform and obviously enjoying his sense of power, his stamp, his slow computer.

He looked down at his shoes, counted to ten before he approached the counter with his fist clenched in the pocket of his jacket.

The rest one could read about in the newspapers the following day but all I can say is that it slipped out of his hand, he lost his head and had to use all his diplomatic ingenuity to replace it more or less properly back on his torso. It might not have looked pretty but it wouldn't have been possible to do a nicer job; a shredded head of red cabbage on a stick.

*

Today he works at a field office in Ethiopia where he assists in archiving reports he wrote in the past in a gigantic hangar built by the locals and financed by the rest of the world.

He walks down the rows of steel shelves with file boxes, letting his finger run across the coarse surface of cardboard. He straightens a tag and lets his gaze follow the 400 meter long shelf to the back wall. The whole place is lit by fluorescent tubes, the temperature is precisely 20 degrees. He thinks it looks beautiful and then he feels he's making a difference, maybe that's why he smiles, he is still contributing to making the world a slightly better place, of that he is convinced.

He opens the sliding door to Ethiopia's hot reality and steps out into the desert. It looks like it's going to be another cloudless day.

The Noble White One

Oh, how well I remember them, the happy aid workers placed behind tall fences in the middle of some destitute area, endowed with guards, nannies, cleaning personnel, female cooks and a mantra about the distribution of wealth. There isn't talk of exploitation or supremacy, let's just get that straight right away, it's a question of giving aid, doing a good deed and how it's always been done. Changing it would be close to impossible, it would mean resisting the local rules of the game. Well, maybe not entirely impossible , but it would send the wrong message.

There is a concerned wrinkle on the red forehead.

Otherwise don't mention the mission, for God's sake, not a word about its usefulness. Cars, on the other hand, servant girls, shopping malls where you can buy chocolates that haven't been lying on a wheelbarrow in the hot sun. Which girls, m/w, you have screwed, which girls you want to screw, which girls you can screw without having to worry about getting HIV. A judicious Trinity, the servant girl who is a virgin, you take her for a ride in your four-wheel-drive, at a fast speed down bumpy dirt roads so that the old timer in the back will be forced to ditch her earthenware so that she can concentrate on keeping a firm grip, now that's what you call fun! You should have seen the look in her eyes, that bearded face of hers in a complete panic as the iron cow roared away. She may have regretted the short lift she had so quietly been begging for with upturned eyes and her scrawny arms stretched forth toward the body of the truck.

And then you just had to screw the servant girl, right after letting the bearded oldie off at a clay hut by Victoria Lake, up against the monkey-bread tree in the heat of the high noon where the grass is shimmering and red dust is swirling around your feet, or is that just a cliche? In which case, should the jumping Masai also be removed from the story, their naked legs and flaming red woolen outfits? They walk slowly past us in the background with long, dragging strides, driving a herd of goats in front of them with long sticks. A dog barks.

It could also be at the big hotel, so dizzyingly close to falling into the Indian Ocean, that the only thing keeping it up there is international aid money and corruption. But there you might lose your thoughts in the hopelessly big moon pulling itself out of the water, old-fashioned and daftly yellow, and that damn servant girl is starting to feel more like a millstone around your neck with her clumsy manners and ascetic attitude, with her virginity that has to be removed in order to live up to the distorted image of the White Noble One. It suddenly feels heavy and involved, sort of like the office job in Silkeborg you left not that long ago.

Behind the hotel are two telephone poles from the last election, you don't notice them until now, they were put there to make up for the lack of campaign posters, as a promise of the improvements that never came. You consider climbing up one of them, perhaps allow yourself to fall down on the ground with a thud, the ground consisting of cracking red soil that in a different part of the world becomes houses, villas, castles with oriels and frills, but first bricks that prior to then can be dropped from great heights onto the heads of Jutlandish farmer boys.

BRICKS

John and Kent were the troublemakers of the class. John was big and coarse and would hesitate a little before landing a blow. He had a hint of intelligence hidden behind his iris, but a somnolent gleam covered his eye, giving it a matte finish. His movements were heavy even though he tried to make them lighter so that he could keep up with his eternal companion. Kent was little and skinny, he would hit you without hesitation, answered without thinking first and would let people laugh if what he answered had been wrong once again. Or gave them a slap if there were no grown-ups around.

Their approach to soccer said just about everything. John was the best in the class for making a long-range shot and Kent was the best dribbler in the class. You would see him disappear into a throng of players on the opposite team to emerge on the other side unscathed with the ball still stuck between his feet. Then he would deliver it to John who would hammer the ball, making it sing across the stadium.

*

Kent had four older brothers from whom he presumably had learned all his bad habits. They were the terror of the town when together they came cruising into the local hang-out on their scooters with their long hair, fringed jackets and bad attitudes fluttering in the wind. They would gather on the corner to drink soda, smoke cigarettes and stare hard at whomever happened to pass by. They seldom ever spoke to each other but then again there wasn't much to talk about, was there?

They lived out in the country where their father owned a mason firm of the more questionable kind. It was a family business, that is to say, the brothers would give a hand and earn some pocket money which they could spend on booze and cigarettes if they wanted to.

They had changing mothers and it was seldom that their father was home. The sons were often seen running the business even though they weren't supposed to officially, but you couldn't just let things come to a standstill just because their father wasn't at home. He instructed them in what to do before he left. The oldest of the remaining brothers acted as a shift boss for the others which for the most part worked just fine. Until one day when things went wrong.

Kent was busy collecting some stones in the courtyard when one of his brothers emptied a wheelbarrow full of bricks right on his head from the second floor. Perhaps it was a primitive kind of practical joke, perhaps it was an accident, perhaps it was an act of revenge for when Kent ruined his bicycle a few weeks earlier. At any rate, he now lay lifeless under a pile of bricks in the courtyard.

*

Birger was the one who told us about the accident. Birger was our homeroom teacher, newly graduated from Copenhagen, complete with a mustache which he had grown in order to look a little older, and his open a's. He was one of us and we quickly accepted him even though he introduced us to some singing games and anti-authoritarian ideas that were on the progressive side. He didn't think it was necessary for us to line up in two rows in front of his door for his classes or wait to sit down until he entered the classroom.

After a few months he grew a beard.

He would usually be whistling or humming when he entered the classroom but on that day he entered quietly and positioned himself in front of the blackboard. Normally he would have thrown his bag over into the corner and shouted something or other to a random pupil. Today he placed his bag by his feet and quietly said:

"Kent won't be coming for a while. He has been the victim of an industrial accident."

He sounded as though he were about to cry. A fly was buzzing around his head but he didn't try to swat it like he would on an ordinary day. We reacted more to his mood than to the message itself. The class was completely silent.

"I don't know much more than you do," he said, running his thumb and index fingers through his mustache. That was the first unpleasant message he had to deliver to the class, and he had had to take a deep breath before entering the classroom that day. Even though Kent had been a handful for him, no one would ever wish for one of one's pupils to get a barrowload of rocks poured down on his head.

Kent had been driven to the emergency room by his oldest brother who could, of course, drive the flat bed truck even though he didn't quite have his driver's license yet. He was 15. They didn't know where their father was and it was in the days before cellular phones but they had managed to maneuver their lifeless little brother into the passenger seat while the other three jumped up onto the truck body and the fourth one got the engine started. It took a while before they found the hospital, they had never been there before, but they finally found it and Kent was immediately taken to the Intensive Care Unit where he remained for the next two weeks. They sewed him together, stuck tubes and wires into him that had to breathe for him, feed him and measure his condition. After a week he gained consciousness whereupon he was able to lie there staring into space with his big eyes or at the monitor that reported his pulse. Every afternoon some of his brothers would come visit him, sometimes also his father, but even though he looked forward to their coming he looked just as much forward to their leaving. They were used to being physical with each other, as opposed to talking or showing compassion.

When he returned to school after several months he was unrecognizable. For one thing his long hair was gone, but it wasn't so much that. He was wearing a Massey-Ferguson cap and if we asked him to he would remove it and show us all the scars that formed a strange map on the top of his head. He had been given 47 stitches on his head alone he said, but when we asked him what it had been like at the hospital he would be evasive.

"Just fine," was all he would say.

It wasn't so much that, it was more that he had become so quiet and meek. He still didn't do his homework but now he would try to give an answer if he was asked about something and would get embarrassed if he couldn't answer correctly. John tried to revive the friendship, the dynamic duo, but that didn't work either. It was as though something had been broken inside of Kent. As though the rocks had hit and shut off a switch in his mind.

On a rare occasion he would participate in soccer, but he would gasp for breath and constantly lose the ball, so he gave up on that, too, just like we not so long afterward gave up on him.

Six Half Open-Face Sandwiches

He remembers the time when he himself attended school. The time when he would get six half open-face sandwiches with liver pate in his lunch bag every day, back when you did as the teacher said, back when everything in the world was in proper order, ditches with trickling water, stewed apples every Friday, cherry trees that gently released their white blossoms into the wind in front of the principal's residence, and ah, to run through that white carpet of snow on your bare feet. Back when a lash across the back of his hand by the math teacher went wrong and broke his index finger as a result. It grew together crookedly and during the winter the extreme tip of his finger still hums, bringing back memories of his school days. He can't remember anymore why he was hit, but he is pretty certain that he deserved it.

He holds up his hand in front of him and looks at the finger pointing at a hopeless angle, a little to the left, as though there is nothing worth pointing to straight ahead of him. It points at the drops running down the shower curtain, they hit his shoulder, spraying onto the shower curtain where some of them remain like little buds while others grow heavy and run down, melting together into bigger drops, running faster than the others, down toward the floor. It is fascinating, an image of something he is unable to decipher. Drops that run, time that passes, his naked shoulder and body? He looks down at himself, down at his liver spots, pigmentary changes and drooping skin, down at his decline. It all is connected. He was once a handsome man, he is almost certain of that.

Back then there was respect for authorities, not like today where people are only interested in themselves, and no one respects anything, is that what it is? He turns off the water and lets reality enter the room, the neighbor is clattering with the kitchen utensils on the terrace next door, half-stifled sounds are coming from the living room, the wind is whistling through the half-open window. He turns on the radio that reports a rocket attack in Gaza, a man that went berserk in an airport in Kuala Lumpur, a middle aged woman who called the police because there wasn't anymore toilet paper at a public toilet where she sat taking a shit, a world out of joint.

He dries himself and goes into the bedroom where he gets lost in his thoughts by the window. He lives across from a dorm and can look right inside the small cubicles that make up the students' homes. Some of the students are playing soccer on the lawn outside, in the sun, busy wasting their time, their possibilities, their lives. It won't be long before they'll be the ones standing up there looking down at the impossible youth, isn't it stupid?

Yet still he whistles, he catches himself whistling.

Sometimes he can see the young girls coming out from the shower over there. They don't consider drawing the curtains, but let him stand there gaping, indignant and titillated, as though they are taking pleasure in it. He is completely convinced that they are taking pleasure in it, that they are doing it deliberately, as a kind of revenge. Even though they have no idea in what direction their nipples are pointing, their skin effortlessly holding them together, even though they are a bit too fat, plump, in fact, everything glistening and quivering. He is contradicting himself, he knows that. Everything is kept together in contradictions, he thinks to himself as well, the world is comprehended in dialectical terms. something along those lines. Right now the world is good and smiling and they are bathing in sultry attention, assuming that that is how it is for everyone and that is how it will always remain.

He knows them. That is, he doesn't know them personally, that's not what he's thinking, but he has worked as a teacher for 26 years now so he knows them, their narrow horizons, expensive clothes and polished nails. They used to flirt with him, his pupils, lean forward so that he couldn't help seeing their tanned cleavages, but that doesn't happen so much anymore. Now they come too late to class, flinging the door open while talking on their cell phones, polishing their nails in class, the stench of solvent and acetone giving him headaches and making him nauseous. He can't stand it, but he knows that it'll only get worse if he comments on it, that'll just mean that more of them will start painting their nails the following days, or hiding their open bottles of nail polish remover in order to sit in their chairs and observe his torment like little predators just waiting for their prey to expose itself. He feels that the only way he can stifle their provocation is by ignoring them, no one listens to what he says in class anyway, so there's nothing for him to lose. And his self-respect is something he lost a long time ago.

Now it's just a matter of holding out, make up things to say in order to fill up the time he has left in class without anyone discovering that his words no longer make any sense. That they presumably never made sense, because how can you refer to something that doesn't exist?

And so he has to go home and lie down, wash down the headache pills with a glass of cheap wine. Sometimes he remains sitting in the teacher's room staring into space. He doesn't know what is going through his mind. It's as though his body shuts down and he knows that the others are talking about him, but what can he do? He is no longer in control of his body, there is a tingling sensation in his arm, his eyes are spacey, his legs have fallen asleep.

Maybe they feel sorry for him, maybe they'd like to help him but don't know how? Those are some of the thoughts he sometime gets as he sits on his chair in the teacher's room, alone, he has to think about something to keep from going crazy.

Once again, the mumbling sounds coming from the living room, the scraping sound of a chair being pulled across the floor and he shouts whether she might be more quiet. It's seldom that he has any guests over, the neighbors might wonder about it, he can no longer remember how loud you are supposed to speak in an apartment.

He finds some clothes in a closet: brown corduroy pants, a striped polo shirt, dark blue tennis socks, and he sits down on the bed and puts them on. He has a back pain, the small of his back has frozen, so it takes some time, especially the socks because he has to sort of catch his toes with the opening of the sock like you would a fish with a very small net.

He can hear something topple over in the living room. The floor lamp?

When he is fully dressed he goes into the kitchen and puts up some coffee. He straightens up the standing lamp on his way, that was what had toppled over. He checks to see whether it is still working. It is.

He finds coffee beans in the freezer, grinds some coffee, pours it into the espresso pot which was expensive, gets it started. He loves the smell of coffee, almost more than its taste. When he thinks of all the bad cups of coffee he's drunk in the teacher's room he almost can't bear it. He can practically feel it splashing around in his stomach as the manifest proof of 26 years of battle in the school system.

He skims the cream off the milk, pours the coffee on top of it so that a little happy face can be discerned in the foam. He smiles back at it, not until then does he look over at her, catches her gaze and continues to smile. He has always gone out of his way to ensure there was a good atmosphere in his classes. It's hard to learn anything in an unsafe environment.

She is sitting on his favorite chair in the middle of the living room and he is practically taken by surprise when he discovers that her hands are tied behind her back and her feet to the legs of the chair. A corner of his memory can suddenly recall how she got there, but it isn't a corner he uses that often. He really has to strain himself and he squints and takes a sip of coffee. And I'll be darned if she doesn't also have a gag in her mouth and mascara is running down her cheeks. It doesn't look good, he has to admit, not good at all.

"I dreamed that a cat had eaten my face," she says in a tone so calm and trustworthy that it's almost impossible to believe that just a few minutes ago she was naked, that her big breasts were flying around the whole living room, hitting both the wall and the ceiling that left big, oval marks, toppled over the laundry rack and the pile of newspapers.

"At first it started scratching me with its little claws, ever so carefully, so blood started trickling out, and now that I'm talking about it, I realize that I must have been looking at myself from the outside because there is no doubt in my mind that I was the one lying there and I was the one who saw it." .

She takes a sip of her tea and pushes the rocking chair back so that it starts rocking back and forth with her as a seemingly unresisting passenger, her thighs that rise when her heels hit the ground with a careful bump. But she is the one rocking it and she closes her eyes and gives in to it or recalls the dream about the cat that ate her face, what do I know?

I get up, staring up at the ceiling with eyes wide open. Fetch the bowl of sweet biscuits and place it in front of her, smile as I try to avoid the memory of her ass pressed against my balcony door, crushed flat against the floor, staring up toward the ceiling with its wide open eye.

"It finally ate my face, very slowly, almost with delight and I didn't make any protest. I just don't know whether it means anything."

"I doubt that it does," says the man who comes out of

my bathroom wearing my bathrobe. He is still steaming and his hair is dripping on the terry cloth until he takes the towel he is holding in his hand and wraps it around his head. He laughs, baring his white teeth and pink gums, letting out a hawk-like sound.

"You have a wonderful bathtub," he says as he turns toward me. "Thank you for letting me borrow it, for letting us borrow your apartment at all."

I nod. The image of his big cock that toppled over the weeping fig as he turned around, hitting the stereo bench, leaving phallic marks on her pale skin when he lost his balance and fell.

She gives the rocking chair one last push which makes her practically lie in a horizontal position in the air, and the movement is for some reason depicted in slow motion; her eyes that open slowly, look up at the ceiling, her thighs that are pulled down toward the weave of the chair, her breasts that gently lap against her neck.

I know your flight, you flying wave.

"We have to be going anyway," she says as she puts time back in its normal rotation, the chair that lands in an upright position. She gets up and brushes a few crumbs off her dress. "I had such a pleasant time."

I escort them out to the hallway and open the door, wave somewhat awkwardly at them before quietly closing the door and go back to the living room where I raise the weeping fig back up, straighten its leaves, fetch a kitchen cloth and wipe off the worst of the spots. Whereupon I sit down in the rocking chair. I drink the last of her tea and tilt the chair carefully back. I can still feel her warmth, her scent, close my eyes and give in to the chair's rhythmic. Processing. The loss of her.

I don't see it, none of what he shows me, not the stainless steel, the rustic table, the expensive wallpaper. I listen to him but can't make reality match his words. Instead I see the old dining table where father broke my arm with the iron girder. I see the entrance hall where he hit me hard with my school books because I had forgotten them on the bench. And I especially see the eyes from the innermost room, behind the kitchen, that followed my every move when we ate. They were glowing eyes in the darkness that belonged to a child who was always being excluded.

My half brother wasn't allowed to eat his meals with us, instead he would be banished to a small storage room in the attic. He would usually get the same to eat as we did, but not always. If he had behaved exceptionally badly he would get porridge or bread, that's how I remember it, once in a while nothing at all. My father's new wife couldn't handle him and gave my father an ultimatum: If my half brother ate together with us she wouldn't. She wasn't going to tolerate being made a fool of every night, it had to do with the teasing tone that he used that she heard in everything he said, his lack of respect. It came down to a choice between child and lover and my brother was sent to the attic.

He was older than me and when I was twelve he was finally sent to boarding school but he left his eyes hanging out there in the attic. That's still how I remember him, a pair of eyes that followed my movements at the dining table. Not his voice, not his arms embracing me, not our conversations at night after we had been put to bed. There were years when we slept in the same room and we must have spoken with one another then? ?

I remember the feeling of not doing anything and how much it hurt to be praised or caressed while he was looking. I remember how his eyes could practically burn a hole in my cheek, the sense of pain but also of a secret bond the others didn't feel or know anything about.

*

I met him by accident some years ago at an exhibition preview at my cousin's. She was the only member of our family with whom he had maintained contact because she had also broken off with her family and was struggling to get her life to work.

He was an entrepreneur, everything from pacifiers, water filters and currency exchange to alternative jewelry and news sites that wanted to revolutionize the way in which we follow the news. He told about the whole thing with enthusiasm and it was odd standing across from him and not feeling any sort of connection other than a phantom pain. It was like attending an entrepreneur seminar where your brother is the keynote speaker.

He was honest about his feelings in conversation, if you didn't get too close. He was clearly accustomed to working with them in order to connect emotionally with his customers so he could make a sale. That means investing yourself in the projects.

"My only goal was to get rich," he said, "that was what drove me. To prove that I was worth something, money gives you the opportunity to be carefree."

"And have you succeeded?" I asked, smiling.

"In what?"

"In becoming rich and carefree, of course."

"You can never get too rich," he said a little curtly. My cousin had told me that he was a multi-millionaire and wouldn't have to work anymore for the rest of his life. But that he couldn't stop working, because what would he do then? He had had several relationships, but they never lasted for more than a few weeks, and no children.

"Do you have any children?" I asked, "Have I become an aunt?"

"Not as far as I know."

"I have a boy of seven but am no longer together with his father."

"Oh, OK."

It was difficult for him to handle me, increasingly difficult. I was a stranger who could potentially threaten his well-organized world. So he continued talking about all his successes which I let him do. He was wearing a brown suit that looked good on him, his posture was erect. He resembled that which he was, a successful businessman until I plucked up my courage and met his gaze. It was the same gaze as back then, I don't know what I had expected. His eyes had changed, of course, had grown bigger and emptier, but his gaze was the same and it hit me right in the pit of my stomach, across time, and I extended my hand to him. He took a step back, so I got up. I got up from the dinner table and went up to the attic where I squatted down next to him. I fumbled for his hand and he let me hold it.

That's how we sat for a while, without saying anything, holding each other's hands.

FISH

They would usually go on fishing trips together. Without saying a word they would sit in the boat and watch the ripples spread in the water where the hooks penetrated the mirror, the clouds floating quietly across the sky, across the water, the sound of a fish tail on the surface nearby, a dragonfly that landed in the stern or swirled around their motionless silhouettes. He was good at being quiet, they were good at being quiet together, the father and son, floating in a little boat on a smooth mirror of water. It was the closest to happiness he had been so far.

He had always enjoyed fishing, as a child he would use it as an excuse to be alone. They lived close to the ocean and after school he would often pack his fishing bag and bike down to the harbor where he would sit at the very edge of the jetty and catch eel pouts, later flat fish and real eels, every now and then a cod, garfish when it was the season for it. It had helped him get through his childhood, the calmness, and being good at something, having a secret pact with the ocean itself, a pact with Neptune.

He recognized the various species of fish. He read books about fish and subscribed to *Field and Stream* when he turned ten, and when he thought back on his childhood he saw himself either sitting there on the jetty holding the fishing rod or lying on the green-flecked plank bed in the guest room reading about angler stories in the pale yellow glow of the night lamp.

He could now recognize himself in his son, recognize

his childhood's state of mind and he wanted to equip him with the tools needed to tackle things like melancholy and the feeling of being alone in the world.

He gave him a good starter's kit when he turned four years old and it was good for practicing but he regretted having been so stingy the first time they went out to the lake to try it out. The sound of the wheel that ticked in the wrong way as his son reeled in the hook jarred in his ears when the line ran out. Shortly afterward he went out and purchased a better fishing kit that could be used for most things, still with a fixed spooling reel, but with an integrated gearbox and a stronger brake. Later they went shopping together and bought deep sea reel, fly reel and carp reel and rods that matched.

He had a stressful job that included a lot of traveling so he was grateful that they could share this passion of his. He could spend time with his offspring without it feeling like an irksome duty. He loathed sitting at a playground having to look at wailing children who wasted one's time, he had to admit that. On the ocean, on the other hand, he felt that he came into his own as a father when he helped hooking the worms or killing the fish, virtues that turned a boy into a man and connected him with nature.

Yet, still it was as though the boy resisted. Sometimes he had the sneaking suspicion that the boy would have preferred not to catch anything at all. He noticed that the boy would give a start when there was a tug in the line, that he would retreat when the fish had landed at the bottom of the boat and was fighting its last impossible battle against the air, quivering in cramps when it was hit with the final merciful blow. In the beginning he had at least pulled the hook out himself, cut off the head, played with the eyes of the fish, now he would gasp for air as though he was on the verge of getting an anxiety attack as the fish broke through the surface and landed in their world.

"Are you sure you don't want to do it yourself?" he asked, to which the son would shake his head violently.

"I have a headache," or "I feel nauseous, Dad." He had made an attempt at one point but was forced to stop in the middle of it because he had to throw up which he did right on the fish's head.

"You can't strangle them, they live underwater."

*

One day things went seriously wrong. He had managed to hook a big rainbow trout with a stainless steel salmon hook with Powerbait and together they had struggled to get it into the boat. He had to take over the rod which was actually too thin for such a big fish. It demanded all his years of experience to bring it to its death, it would have been a catastrophe if it had slipped away. In moments like these, the meaning of life was momentarily condensed, life and death literally depended on his coordination and timing. He gave his son the landing net which he held ready by the water's edge.

"Wait a second," the father hissed,"it has to go in under her, you risk pushing her off the hook."

When they had landed it, the son fell backward in the boat and hit his head against the paddock, he lay completely pale and bleeding from a gash in the back of his head, a little bit of vomit coming out of his mouth, meanwhile the fish had escaped the hook and jumped into a lake of scales and slimy liquids around him.

His response was for the most part rational, he rushed back to land, managed to step on the fish, lifted the boy's head and started the outboard motor. He carried him up to the house where his wife came running from the kitchen. She must have seen them coming up the garden path from the lake, it was Sunday. The boy was still lifeless, but he could feel that his body was quivering like a dying fish.

His wife took over the lifeless bundle without saying a word, just looked at him and extended her arms to receive him. She took the car keys down from the hook, went out to the car where she buckled the boy up, got in and drove off. The whole thing happened in what felt like one movement. He was left standing there watching the car, the emptiness inside him growing.

*

It was discovered that the boy had fish allergy. It had a Latin name which he couldn't recall, the only thing he could recall was his wife's reproachfulness in her intonation as she said it. But the boy had developed an allergy against fish, of course he had. He could have died his wife explained, it was actually nothing less than a miracle that he had survived. From now on he wasn't to have any direct contact with fish. He struck an attitude of suspicion, but that was just the way things were, she said. That was what the doctor had said, so there was absolutely no getting around it.

A few days later she bought an aquarium with four brightly colored fish as a compensation for the loss, but that was just silly, he thought. It was like inviting the enemy in, it swam around observing him, basking in the attention or sucking on the stones only to spit them out later with an empty look in its eyes. Luckily the boy couldn't tolerate them either, just like he could get sick if any of their dinner guests had had tuna fish for lunch.

He thought it was irritating that the boy had turned out to be such a softie, and as close as he had felt to him out there on the boat, he felt equally estranged from him now. Sitting there with his pale face, the dark circles under his eyes, staring at him. Or whispering a guilt ridden goodnight to him in his hoarse voice. Demonstratively.

Sometimes he would eat salmon for lunch and it would give him an odd sense of satisfaction seeing his son having to gasp for breath when he came home from school. He knew it wasn't right, but it was kind of fun. He also started fishing again, he had to make an effort to hold on to the things that mattered to him and not let the boy determine everything in his life. He hid the fishing equipment down by the lake and gave the fish he caught to business associates and good friends who promised to be discreet about it. Sometimes he would grill the fish out on the island before coming home whereupon the son would put on a show like you've never seen before. It was all unbearably theatrical, he felt. The son never said anything, he suffered in silence, which was almost worse, the reproachful, swimming eyes.

*

One night he dreamed about that day in the boat but some of the roles had been switched around: He had been himself, but the fish had been the boy and the boy the fish. In the dream he clearly saw himself stepping hard on the boy's face on his way over to help the fish, saw his one eye fall out of its eye socket, saw him floundering about at the bottom of the boat before finally growing completely still.

The next morning he went on a business trip. On the one hand he wanted to check and see that the boy was okay, on the other he could hear the soft sound of the taxi engine outside, the gravel under its tires in the driveway. He felt light and clear-headed and could almost taste the mild morning air even before entering the driveway. Somewhere in front of him an animal was croaking in the thicket, a frog or a cuckoo, he really didn't care. He unbuttoned the top button of his shirt, hesitated a little and looked across the lake before getting into the taxi and nodding to the driver who nodded back reservedly.

"Whereto?" he asked. He had a calming voice.

And the Cuckoo Shall Cuckoo

Some people thought she was beautiful, which I no longer understand but then my clearest memory of her is from the day in the forest when she collapsed, her long neck that sort of broke before her entire figure disappeared down in the fog. The image of the red flower on her stomach, her long fair hair spread across the moss.

She looked like a vulture with that long neck of hers and her curved back and cold eyes. She had a voice which was nasal and shrill and she would make diligent use of it if there were interesting people close by, people with power, people who could be used. Then she would be a good listener, act politely, be vivacious and there was no end to the anecdotes she could tell. Most of them had to do with exciting people she knew (well) and the exotic places they had been together (Lisbon, Istanbul, Cape Town), a few of them had solely to do with herself.

She could hold an entire crowd in the palm of her hand and in breathless suspense alone by telling about herself and her famous friends. She was the perpetual motion machine of the party who could piss itself in the mouth, the false inference of the party: She was interesting because she had interesting friends who were interesting because they knew her.

She had originally been a musician but now she was also publishing poems, curating exhibits and appeared on television as an expert. She could talk about mostly anything, you had to give her that, and she always gave her opinion, whatever the conversation happened to be about, whether it was the conflict zones of the world, the latest Danish rock band that proved to be as hopeless as the others or the government's image problems.

She could also be silent and she could roll her eyes if a newly minted poet happened to be off in his description of himself or the world, send knowing glances to her friends across the table if such individuals were in her presence, on an evening at a sidewalk cafe in the city center where the coolness of the early autumn caused blankets to be placed on chairs and people could see their breath in the air for the first time. Or she could retreat within herself and wait until the whole thing had passed, sit very quietly with her impenetrable green eyes, hunched over and saving her energy for more important projects, peeling candle wax off the table with her polished fingernails or the label off of a bottle.

She could also leave, few could leave a gathering the way she could, so that no one was in doubt that she had left. Even after she had left her presence continued to manifest itself.

She had attended the music academy, did I mention that? And worked together with famous musicians of all genres. Name any prominent musician and she would have a story from the rehearsal room ready.

*

Many men were crazy about her, of course they were, she was specially designed to be coveted. They talked about her irresistible charm and sexy voice, how they wouldn't mind screwing her. In consequence, she dated around quite a bit and considered herself to be in love with most of her affairs. They confirmed to her that she had feelings and in return they would get sex and a corner of her cape of fame which they could parade with around town after she had dumped them. Perhaps they could sew a handkerchief from it, a fez or a cuff link, because it wasn't bigger than that, after all.

But then the most wondrous thing happened, she fell in love with an exceptionally unexceptional man. She couldn't explain it; it was a physical attraction which she had never experienced until now. It took her completely aback, just like she was surprised by the strength of her own feelings. As mentioned above, she thought what she had been experiencing before had been love. He was naive, said all the wrong things and was unable to conceal his uninhibited fascination with her which was always unbecoming. Still, her pulse beat faster, her mouth would grow dry as she saw him before her in her mind, naked on his bed at home, pleasant-smelling, groomed and holding his big cock in his hand. She then tried to imagine what he would do with it afterward and was shocked by how banal it was, how banal she was.

He was an engineer and worked at Copenhagen Water Supply or Hofor as it is now called. He talked about it without sounding like a boring engineer, with self-irony and a sense for the significant things. He smiled and looked down at the table every time he said something about himself. His upper arms were suntanned and toned, the muscles coiled under the surface of his skin.

At the end of the evening they kissed across the table, later next to each other on the bench. For a brief moment she saw the whole thing from the outside, herself utterly uncool and not all there, the others who were smiling and had probably seen it all coming long before she had, the empty beer bottles on the table, a heavy old man in the corner that stared at them uninhibitedly, loud, drunk voices, the fight that was brewing, the laughter. Then she buried herself in him once again.

She shrugged it off when she met the others the following days. She admitted that she had kissed the engineer but put up smokescreens as to what had happened later that night and passed it off as a moment of drunk impulsiveness on her part. And couldn't there be room for that as well? It had been yet another fine anecdote, but nothing more than that. He was an engineer so it went without saying that nothing was ever going to come of it. And had they heard what he had said about the newest Danish authors? She had had to restrain herself to keep from laughing.

Even though it was clear as day that she couldn't be seen with him she would still get an urge whereupon her fingers would sort of call him on the phone of their own accord after a party, and pretty soon they had become night lovers. After a while that too grew and she spent most of her weekends with him. They took long walks holding each others' hands, vacationed at inns by the North Sea and went to the movies together. They were unbearably petit bourgeois but she allowed herself to enjoy it. Every now and then they would have his ordinary friends over for dinner and they even visited his parents. It was supposed to look coincidental, just a short stop on the drive to Northern Zealand but she could sense that there was more to it. The parents lived in a small detached house where the backyard bordered on Hareskoven, his mother wore a sailor sweater and served tea from a blue fluted ceramic pot, his father smoked a pipe.

*

Of course it became increasingly evident to him that they had different expectations for the relationship, he wasn't stupid. For example he would have liked to have gone with her to the concerts and readings she attended because he was interested in her and therefore also in her professional work. He understood why he couldn't come with her to the VIP parties but why not to an exhibition preview, if he kept in the background?

"It just wouldn't be a good night for that," she would explain, he had to understand that. Which he did. She, in turn, would call him in an excited state at four o'clock in the morning.

"I'm on my way to your place, Honey," she'd practically shouted in the phone. "And I want sex."

"Uh, OK," he'd say tired and flattered. On the one hand he didn't have the energy for it, on the other he could feel his cock growing bigger under the blanket, as though it had fathomed something he hadn't. He got up. Washed up and swirled some toothpaste around in his mouth. She didn't like it when he smelled too much of sleep.

He wasn't really the jealous type, yet still he felt a pang when she would go out at night without him. He knew how other men looked at her and didn't know her well enough to know how she responded to them. She sensed his sprouting jealousy and took full advantage of it, telling him in detail the kinds of compliments she had received, how many kisses on the cheek and lustful glances, even direct offers of sex, imagine that!

When he had the energy for it he would manage to change her mood. He would start a pillow fight, tickle her or carry her to bed, forcing her to surrender. But she could also make herself go stiff in his arms, insist on being lowered and then he would feel like a naughty boy as he placed her aggrieved body on the floor.

Once they ran into one of her friends on the street, whereupon she quickly let go of his hand and positioned herself at a meter's distance away from him.

"That's the engineer," she would say, introducing him after a while. They'd laugh a little at that.

*

He lived in a three-room apartment on Christianshavn on the canal with a built-in bookcase and a terrace roof. He had many books, read a wide range of them but still managed to draw the wrong conclusions. Sometimes he would try to start a conversation about a book or an article he had read in the Sunday paper. He felt that that dimension was lacking in their relationship.

"Did you read how the minister of Cultural Affairs is giving prior warning of a possible confrontation regarding future support for the arts?"

But she didn't bother to answer him. The best thing was just to ignore him, it would usually pass of itself then. His petty opinions were a huge turn off to her, as long as he kept his mouth shut their relationship was as close to perfect as it could get.

"Did you read, there's a UN employee who went berserk in an airport in Kuala Lumpur because he felt he wasn't being treated fairly."

"Yeah, that's funny."

He had a large banana palm tree and originally designed furniture.

*

They would both go hunting. That was how they got engrossed in a conversation that evening, talking about the difference between pressure hunting and battue, hunting as an analogy to night life, for example, what kind of hunting methods were being used at the bar in which they sat. He himself preferred deer stalking, he confided to her, where you tiptoe through the terrain solely in search of the best shooting position. It was a matter of being able to decipher nature, the wind, the game and using your intuition.

That was just before he kissed her.

She had obtained a hunting license in order to be able to partake in the big hunts where the more senior members of the cultural elite would meet, he had grown up on a deserted farm where it was natural to hunt, both rodents and for food. They had had a forest that had been big enough for them to be allowed to go hunting in it. Later the family moved into a detached house, but he and his father continued going hunting together and they were both excellent hunters. He had several hunting friends and during hunting season, he would go hunting several times a month.

He had been trying to get her to go hunting with him for a long time, and one day when he was about to go out with some friends she finally caved in. She most likely thought that it couldn't do any harm. And in a way it couldn't. She was the one who was clumsy and shrill, positioning herself with the wind behind her, sniffing the air audibly. She was probably acting the way she always did, but out there it became very visible. And audible. At one point her telephone vibrated through the silence and what made it all the worse was the fact that she tried to defend herself afterward, "But I had turned down the volume, what more could I have done?"

She clearly wasn't impressed with the rest of the hunting group, but she didn't leave, she even stooped to answer them politely when they asked her something and waited until they were sitting in the car on their way home with specifying what was wrong with them all.

*

He also joined her on one of her hunting parties but only because he knew one of the organizers who had asked him to join them. She discovered it too late to be able to prevent it and she herself couldn't back out of it. She tried to persuade him to forget about it but he smiled and said that that was impossible. After the last hunting party his mood had changed, she thought, he no longer tried to talk to her during breakfast, became increasingly withdrawn and would sometimes reject her advances without her being able to determine what the meaning was behind that.

When they arrived at the hunting lodge all her friends were there, the entire hunting cultural Parnass stood ready in their green outfits and inspiring conversation and she winced. Her initial instinct was to duck, perhaps hide on the floor underneath the front seat where she could just squeeze in. She couldn't see how else she was ever going to get through the day and the humiliation of having arrived there with an engineer. She practiced several formulations in her mind to explain why they had come there together, but none of them seemed suitable. The most important thing was to make it clear that they weren't going steady, preferably without having to offend him too much--what wouldn't it do to her reputation and all the dreams the others had had about her if they knew she had given herself away to a public servant.

But none of that became necessary, the day became very different than she had anticipated. They welcomed him warmly, and her reservedly. Apparently he was the party's best marksman, the one who everyone wanted to join and he behaved calmly and assuredly. He had met several of them on other hunts, the rest had heard about him through them. She noticed how the few women that were there accidentally sort of approached him, would ask his advice about something or try to get a tip. In one sense it was nauseating, on the other hand she suddenly saw him with their eyes. If they were able to like him, why couldn't she, too?

For once she had no idea how to act. She was on enemy turf and she had to get the ball back in her court. She chose to behave like a fool by trying to seek attention, cracking off stupid jokes and make him look like an imbecile to win some cheap points. It didn't work, on the contrary, it made her look even more shrill, she could sense that herself and so could he, obviously. The dynamic in their relationship was about to change, he suddenly saw her without the soft tone filter of love, and he saw a crane nervously shifting its feet.

*

The weather was gray and misty and the visibility that day was poor but the organizers agreed that it would soon pass, so of course they had to go out. The forest had adorned its hat with green, the field had flowers in its bosom and somewhere among the trees the cuckoo was calling. It was very idyllic. And it was also enchanting to walk among the tree trunks together, the rifles slung over one's shoulders, chatting the first part of the way and then growing more silent. They walked together but when they reached the stone fence he made a turn without saying a word as she continued in the fog of the thicket.

He didn't see her again until she emerged from the little glade he had been keeping an eye on. He sat motionlessly behind a stone fence. He had a special talent for sensing when the prey would come, it was most likely an instinct, a well-developed form of intuition. The others sat further away, scattered about in the little field where, according to prevalent hunting theory, it was bound to show up, but he could think like a deer, identify with it, feel the little heart of the animal beating in its body. That was why he was the one who always came home with the most prey.

He didn't think about it when she stepped out from the glade. In a way this was most likely what he had been waiting for, it had to be, he trusted his instincts entirely. It might not have been totally by the book and she may not have been the proudest prey in the forest, a little odd with her crane's neck that stuck out in the mist, her stooped figure that stepped on every noisy thing on the forest floor. But she had stepped into his glade so of course it was inevitable.

He placed the gun to his cheek, his eye may have burned, it probably did, and he probably also laughed a little hoarsely, but he had no feeling of hatred. She stepped into his glade so he aimed at the sound in the fog and fired and he heard the bullet hit its target, she hadn't been further than that. Afterward he wasn't sure, but he might possibly also have seen her body fall to the ground like a shadow silhouette in the fog to take off in proud flight, with her neck outstretched and her wings spread.

He was completely calm, sat a for a while listening to her little plaintive whining which slowly faded. . Then he went over and picked her up, the red blood pouring from her chest, down her fashionable camouflage clothes. She lay completely limp in his arms and he carried her back through the forest and carefully placed her in the line of deer that lay in front of the estate.

Somewhere among the trees the cuckoo was calling.

Cuckoo

The cuckoo called, time passed.

Four years later, much has happened since, but all we see is a man standing in a hallway, his hands by his sides. He is apparently looking out the window, but do we know? His head is facing in that direction, his eyes are open. He doesn't move, only a quivering in his left ring finger indicates that he is alive, held together by a general knowledge that he wouldn't be able to keep himself erect if he were dead. Apparently he isn't being kept erect by anything other than his muscles, however that mechanism works, there are no visible ropes, strings or scaffolding around him.

He stands in front of a mirror and he turns his head again, this time toward the mirror, and looks at his own reflection. I'm guessing it's me. It often is.

The Pig

He stands in front of the mirror. He's done with his morning meditation and his Kegel exercises, it all went fine. In the mirror there is a handsome looking man in royal-blue pajamas, gilt edges, graying temples and the corner of his lips turned slightly downward in a sad frown. He's not quite sure whether it's him. He lifts his hand, so does the man in the mirror, except he looks sick, completely pale with dark circles under his eyes, that's not how he remembers himself. He remembers himself as uninhibited, wild, creative, bursting with vitality and energy.

Am I really sick? he thinks.

He runs his hand through his hair and stares angrily at the man in the mirror, making his eyes flash, tries to kiss him, psyche him. King Lear, he thinks, he remembers all of his famous parts, every line, every phrase.

He goes out to the kitchen in his bare feet. Inside the bedroom Birthe is taking deep breaths, on the verge of snoring, the early morning sun casts a pale ray of light across the parquet floor. He puts up the electric kettle, pours a fair amount of Nescafe powder into a mug, spreads some ginger marmalade on a dry roll.

He writes a note to her while drinking his coffee, black, thanks her for a wonderful evening and night but explains that he will have to leave, the treatment starts early and he would like to avoid the morning traffic to Odense. He doesn't know what he'll be faced with but he is grateful for all her support. He couldn't have wished for a better girlfriend. Smiley face? He empties the mug, puts it in the sink, wipes off the crumbs with a wet cloth.

He walks through the living room carrying his polished leather shoes in his hand out into the dark hallway passage where he sits down on a bench and puts them on. He walks down through the hallway and out into the dining hall room, switches on the light above the row of tables closest to him with a click that echoes through the big room. The tables are old, some chairs are hanging crookedly underneath them, others have been placed up on top of the tables. Nevertheless, the floor hasn't been swept, caramel wrappers and yogurt containers lie under the one closest to him, several pieces of paper a little further down, a newspaper has been left on one of the chairs. It's normally strictly forbidden to remove the newspapers from the reading room but he isn't the kind of boss that makes inflammatory speeches about bad upbringing and being considerate of those who will be using the room after you. He treats his fellow humans with respect and merely expects their acknowledgment in return.

He bumps into Irma in the office hallway and inevitably cringes slightly, greets her with a frail voice, "Good morning, Irma, looks good." He smiles bravely. She concentrates on her pail and mop as she moves across the linoleum floor.

"I'm off to Odense now, we'll have to see when they'll let me return."

She nods, mutters something he doesn't quite catch. Good luck?

He lets out a sigh of relief when he finally reaches the

main door to the parking lot and the cold air of early morning. He would have preferred sleeping late but if you're up anyway there is something utterly fantastic about being the first to receive the cold morning embrace of the universe, to breathe in the air. What a gift, he thinks, a voyage of discovery into unknown territory; the pale stars and the pink horizon across the fields, his breath like a small cumulus across the parking lot.

He unlocks the door of the car, an older model blue Peugeot, gets in and starts the engine. This is going to be a good day, he clearly senses that now. The first day with challenges of a completely different kind. He backs out of the parking space, drives out to the main road and turns right toward the highway. He turns on the radio and starts heading toward Århus. They're playing a song he likes, something with a piano and a girl's touching voice.

*

He senses a strong resistance coming from his colleagues, not just now, at the meeting, but in general. He can't explain what it is. They've dropped little hints about him being gone from the office a lot, that everything's a mess when the captain isn't on board the ship, but what had they expected? He has cancer! He is performing in a play where death has the leading role and he, for once, is a mere extra. There is no prompter and the manuscript still isn't finished.

He is good at making analogies, at dramatizing his points.

It started as intestinal cancer but later it spread to his lymph nodes and most recently to his head. He has explained the entire procedure to his colleagues while at the same time insisting on maintaining a normal workday life and seeing to his usual responsibilities at the school. But he had been hoping for more sympathy from their end, something of which he makes no secret. Is it so hard to understand that the treatment has been taxing, that he has no choice but to follow the doctors' orders? He himself is rather impressed with the fact that he has even been able to function normally while receiving chemotherapy and radiation treatment. Nevertheless, he still senses their suspicion, even on a physical level, and this time it grows in the boardroom, takes on a lilac shade, extends its arms and is practically stifling him. Despite the fact that they have only been discussing neutral subjects during the meeting: keys, project week, guest teachers, problem students.

He is sweating profusely, breathing in gasps, coughs and they all look at him.

"I'm afraid I'm going to have to go in and lie down," he says as he wipes his forehead with a paper napkin. "Jørgen will take it from here. I'm very sorry, but I simply don't have any more energy."

It might not have been the wisest decision but he could sense that it would only have been worse had he stayed.

*

"It can't go on like this," the ceramics teacher says. "We can't possibly run a school without a principal."

"I understand your frustration. Don't you think I'm frustrated, too? I didn't exactly want to get sick, you know." His voice cracks and he practically whispers, "But the treatment is working, the prognosis is good."

"How much longer will you be taking this 'treatment'?"

He doesn't like her tone but it is hard to accuse someone of using a certain tone of voice without exposing yourself and opening up unknown flanks, and he dislikes the unknown even more.

He prefers the shine of a young girl's hair.

"Until I'm well again, I assume," he answers sharply, and then a little more gently, "They think another couple of weeks more, but it'll probably take awhile before I'm back to my normal self."

The room is quiet, a teacher reaches across the table for the red coffee pot. The coffee that is then poured into the cup makes a disproportionate amount of noise.

"I want you to know that I really appreciate all your support," he says but no one says anything, no one looks at him.

The gym teacher unfolds a newspaper clipping and places it on the table.

"How do you explain this?" he asks. "It says you are busy putting on a play in Århus? How does that fit into all your treatments?"

He becomes quiet for a while, groping for an answer. He can feel the dizziness coming on again, whether it is due to their distrust or the treatments is hard to say. .

"It's also been incredibly hard," he says. He is on the verge of tears, you can tell by the grainy sound of his voice. "I don't know how I've managed to get through it all." His hands are shaking, in fact, his entire large frame is shaking from the emotion.

"We don't believe in your play acting anymore," the gym teacher says coldly. "There's too much that doesn't add up."

"There's no law against my putting up a play. It says so in my contract, I can go get it right now and show you."

"That's not really the problem, is it?"

"What is, then?"

It grows completely quiet around the table, no one pours any coffee into their cups, no one says anything, most of them are sitting with their hands by their sides, not daring to look up at him or one another. They are looking down at the table or without focus at the school's former principals who are looking back at them from their gilded frames in an attempt to fill them with courage across the ages.

"Do you want me to show you my scar from the operation?" he asks, first quietly and then subsequently more loudly. "Do you really want me to show you my scar?" He gives them a defiant look, as one duelist to another, it's him against the world, Macbeth against the forest of soldiers. Instead of a light sword he holds onto the ribbed border of his sweater.

"Would you believe me then?"

He gets up, making the chair fall over behind him, stands a little looking at them before he strides through the room and out to the hallway. They can hear his footsteps disappearing in the direction of the principal's house growing increasingly faint to finally fade out entirely.

*

He stubbornly insists on continuing his morning rituals, meditating and doing Kegel exercises, a little bit of yoga and stretching afterward. It's more important now than ever. He sits in a lotus position in his royal blue pajamas, drinks some morning coffee with the newspaper turned to the sport's section before him, Arsenal in an away game beat Tottenham. Had he not embarked on a career in the theater world he would have been a soccer player, there is absolutely no doubt in his mind about that. He is able to kick off equally well with either leg.

He still has the board's full support, but it's been very demanding for him. That is where he expends all his sparse energy. Luckily the chief executive is understanding, not to say easy, all you have to do is flatter him a little. It's a cheap price to pay and he's never had any problem feeding the egos of other people to fulfill his own projects. He views it as a barter deal with both parties winning out.

He gets up, does the last of the stretching exercises and gathers up the newspaper at the very last one, folds it and places it on the kitchen table. It's already a little after eleven, he allowed himself to sleep in today. The last pupils went home yesterday and there is a summer party for the colleagues out on the lawn, barbecue food and wine for lunch. One last challenge before the final reward: six weeks vacation to fully recover. The sun is already baking down from a cloudless sky, and they've promised an all-time hot weather record.

He stands in front of his wardrobe for a long time in his bedroom but ends up choosing a pair of light, light-colored pants and a short-sleeved shirt. He considers putting on shorts because that would signal a down to earth and a kind of laid back, one-of-us-attitude but it would probably be taken the wrong way by his suspicious colleagues. He really does think that his legs have gotten thinner, but they might not be thin enough. They probably expect them to be as thin as if he had just been released from a concentration camp, and he's dead tired of all their ambiguous compliments of how healthy he looks, how quickly he seems to have recovered, that it's a miracle that he hasn't lost more hair, hasn't grown thinner or weaker.

He just needs to get the day over with.

When he comes out on the lawn, several teachers are already standing next to the grill and chatting. The ceramics teacher is busy salting the pig that is turning on the spit. One of them says something and the others laugh out loud. Then they catch sight of him, a light figure approaching them from the opposite side of the lawn. The media teacher lifts his hand and smiles, starts heading toward him, the others continue talking.

"Well, guess we should open a beer, shouldn't we, now that the principal has arrived," one of them says. They enter the kitchen together.

He greets the ceramics teacher exuberantly who is left standing alone by the grill, and the others when they return with a clanging cool bag. He takes a beer and ignores the media teacher who asks if that's really a good idea.

All the men are wearing shorts, he notices, the women short dresses.

They drink some beer and he tries to relax even though the mood is still tense. It's not that anyone says anything, he can just feel it. Several of the male teachers have taken off their shirts and are running around slightly intoxicated on the lawn bare-chested, one of the female teachers has also removed her top and is playing Frisbee with some of the others just in her bra.

He sits some distance from the grill talking with the media teacher who is trying to get him to relax, to try to beat out the bad atmosphere. but he still feels isolated, trapped in his pants and smooth shirt, challenged and unfree. The sweat is running down his chest, it's already penetrated the fabric where his stomach bulges out, stretching the material. And when the gym teacher comes over and asks whether anyone would be interested in a game of soccer in order to work up a little appetite for the pig he gets up, a little too fast, perhaps, but still with some dignity. There are limits to how much a principal can take from his bratty colleagues. He stands swaying a little back and forth before excusing himself and disappearing into the principal's residence. Once and for all he's going to make all their talking cease, he's going to make them regret all their sarcastic comments, their insinuating suspicion.

*

He's gone for a long time. The girls are still playing Frisbee, the boys are kicking a soccer ball among themselves, as the gym teacher tries to catch it, the ceramics teacher continues rotating the big animal on the grill. It's starting to turn brown, every now and then she pours a little water on it so that the rind will be crispy. But it's as though something's missing, a principal and a conclusion, for example, and imperceptibly one is sucked into the school, through the glass doors to the dining hall, across the tile floor to the hallway passage and through the dark hallway to the principal's residence where the door is standing ajar. The teachers remain outside in the sun, getting happier and more drunk for every minute that passes, their shouts getting louder and their movements increasingly uncoordinated. They manage to hit the ball or catch the Frisbee only every so often now.

Anyway, the door to the principal's residence is ajar and you can push it open inaudibly, tiptoe across the parquet floor to the bathroom where you can hear voices. The principal is standing in front of the bathroom mirror in his undershorts observing himself.

"Are you satisfied now?" he says out loud, lifting his arm to his own reflection in the mirror. "Do you believe me now?" He has completely transformed, he's much more pale and has dark circles under his eyes, his hair bristly, thin and wispy and there are bald spots on his scalps. He should have done this a long time ago, he admits to himself. He looks at his own image with a tired gaze, makes a hollow cough. Then he rummages through the makeup box for some red eyeliner and draws ever so carefully the most impressive scar he's ever seen right across his stomach. That'll get them to stop all their evil talk, he is fairly certain of that. He considers whether to draw up some dots along the sides of the scar but decides against it. The stitches have been taken out, he's healed, he mustn't make any mistakes now, God forbid.

He collects the hair from the sink, a whole handful of it and throws it in the waste bin. Then he gathers the makeup articles, the scissors, the brushes, and puts them carefully back in the suitcase which he carries in and places under the bed. The last place anyone would ever think of looking.

He takes out a pair of shorts from the closet and puts them on, goes out of the apartment and into the hallway. Suddenly he realizes that it is a player's tunnel very clearly, the dark hallway. The light that will hit him in a moment, the applause from the packed stadium.

He jumps a few times in place before opening the door to the dining hall and running out to the others.

The Sun

The same sun. The same sun that made the principal sweat like a pig is now shining upon a young real estate agent with a winning personality which he uses to make sales. It's all connected, nature links up all stories, the wind that blows, the sun that shines, the bird that sings the same song over and over. Of course, it's all connected like pea straw and identical twins, pearls on a string, ants lined up in a row, like an organism with a collective conscious in search of sugar and dead insects, ready to sacrifice themselves for the cause.

The same sun shines on a spotted poisonous snake slithering through a village in Khon Kaen, lazily, but with its senses open, black and white images of rush roofs, palms, birds, the smell of food, of rotten windfalls of fresh blood. It lets its tongue play, feels its own senses growing sharper, its predatory instincts about to strike.

In front of it is warm-blooded prey, an unguarded tidbit, an infant lying on a blanket, a small pulse that is transported through the air in waves and hits reaches its snakeskin, penetrates its muscles, bones to reach its inner ear and brain that processes the impressions and interprets them as food.

It is not evil, it is hungry and it slithers further over to the child, opens its mouth, hisses perhaps, but most certainly lets its teeth sink into the soft skin of the infant without in any way shape or form considering its hunger versus questions of ethical behavior.

It feels nothing.

It tastes nothing.

It opens its mouth, opens its jaws at an impossible angle whereupon it pulls the child into its mouth with great effort by propelling itself forward with its rear teeth.

The Agent

I t's a good day for a real estate agent: The green square
patches of the fields, sprinkled among the corn-brown
and rapeseed- golden ones, piebald dairy cows, the sun
from a partly cloudy sky. The hills, and now the road,
that carefully winds up toward the mill before the long
driveway to the right just after the sign: Fjaltringegaard.

"You will have your very own road sign, not many can
boast of having that!"

She has driven out here together with the real estate
agent, sits listening absent-mindedly to the gravel
crunching under the wheels of his dark blue BMW. She
is perspiring alcohol, had one too many yesterday and
started her day with a bitter. Gammel Dansk? He, on the
other hand, smells faintly of Jojoba, the top button of
his freshly ironed shirt is open, the radio is playing hit
lists which are presented by a cocky DJ using words he
himself isn't able to comprehend and making deliberately
humorous comments.

He places his hand on the gearshift, shifts gears. His
hand is brown and his nails well-groomed. She considers
placing her hand on top of it, a sudden whim, she can
already envision them having sex in the driveway, how
she slides over and sits in his lap, against traffic, unbuttons
his white shirt, draws a white stripe down his tanned
chest with her fingernail. There is something about his
nice-looking facade that both provokes her and at the
same time attracts her.

"Of course, I have no idea whether you even know the
area," he says and she nods.

They get out of the car. He has already shut his car door with a soothing click, smoothed out his shirt as she hesitatingly places her foot down on the fine shingle. She looks up at the house that is practically shouting its white color at them. She takes out a pair of sunglasses from her black purse, puts them on and gets up all in one motion, shuts the door.

"I don't think there can be any doubt that this is Viborg's finest address," the agent says as he points toward the fields, the lake, the golf course. "You can see everything from here: the cathedral, of course, the arboretum with the convent garden behind it, the lakes," he points around to the various things, letting her take in the view.

"It is very impressive," she practically whispers.

"And up here you have some peace and quiet," he says encouragingly, as he points to a rhododendron with humming bees, "the birds and the bees."

"Well, I'm single," she mutters to herself.

He clears his throat.

"Shall we go inside?"

They ascend the marble staircase to the main building, she a few steps behind him. His gait is calming, his shoulders down and his back erect.

"It has been thoroughly renovated. It might not be entirely cheap, but then again you'll get a truly complete apartment. I don't know if you're familiar with the history of the house?"

He has unlocked the front door at his first attempt, she observes his efficient movements, the self-assuredness of his tone of voice and gesticulations. Now they are standing in the hallway among chequered marble tiles, faded green walls with tall panels, big paintings of landscapes, flowers and a sole horseback rider. The agent looks at her as though he is waiting for her to give an answer. There is a winding staircase leading up to the second floor, like a mother-of-pearl white serpentine.

"Sorry?" she says, wiping some pearls of perspiration off her forehead.

"I just asked whether you were familiar with the history of the place?" There isn't any trace of irritation in his voice.

"No, not really," she answers a little reluctantly.

"Its roots go back to the 14th century where there was an estate here. Allegedly a Danish prince is even said to have resided here, but he fell out of favor and had to flee to Germany. Or I might be getting a few stories mixed up," he says, smiling apologetically. "It's not that long ago that I read about its history, the apartments haven't been for sale that long. But that sort of thing never really manages to make much of an impression on me."

She looks out the window and he follows her gaze.

"Yes, there must have been some copyhold farms down there," he says, pointing. "All that land belonged to this farm, all the way down to the town."

"Impressive," she says, nodding absent-mindedly. She senses an insecurity sneaking into his voice. She extends her arm, making a gold watch slide out from the sleeve of her white cardigan and registers that he notices it.

"At any rate, it's certain that a number of influential individuals lived here," he continues, "even an English noble family and most recently the farm has been the private property of the city's absolute wealthiest family. He worked in the clothes industry and without mentioning any names he has managed to build up one of the nation's leading fashion houses from here. He lived alone here until four years ago but has chosen to subdivide the property and construct four luxury apartments here in the main building."

"May I see one of them?" she asks as she turns around toward him for the first time, present. She takes off her sunglasses, her eyes are brown, the pupils very tiny. She shudders.

"Of course."

He walks over to the winding staircase, she follows behind him. He tells her about the apartment, the number of square meters, the view, the rich neighbors. She puts her sunglasses back on.

"And what is most exceptional is that there is no residency requirement," he says as he unlocks a tall door on the second floor. "There are several foreign buyers that are interested, but the owner would prefer to sell to someone who intends to stay here all year round." He takes a step back so that she can enter first.

"Only the best materials have been used to renovate it," he says, "The door is made of mahogany, the floors solid oak."

She lets her hand glide across one of the fillings in the door as a kind of response, then says anyway, "Isn't that new as well?" Her voice is thin, as though she has to make an effort to get it to cross her lips, and she holds on to the door, swaying.

"Yes, I am certain it is."

They step onto the oak parquet floor that creaks. The apartment smells of precious wood and paint.

"It hasn't been properly aired out here," he says as though he is able to read her thoughts, pick up the scent of her mood. He enters a room and opens a window, she follows him, straightens her sunglasses. He stands on his toes to get the window fastener to latch on as she walks around in the room, fiddles with a switch, a built in shelf, a gold framed painting.

"Yes, there is a lot of light coming in here."

She has stopped at the fireplace, stares at its hand-painted tiles, at the accessories set made of cast iron. She doesn't hear that he's through with the window and has caught up with her little attempt at breaking away. She starts when he accidentally pushes one of the iron girders, making it swing toward the stand so that it makes a metallic clanking sound. Perhaps she lets out a small cry, at any rate, he gives her a surprised look.

"I'm sorry," he says. They look at one another, there is something both strange and at the same time attractive about the situation, something transgressively intimate. He could be a murderer, she thinks, he could rape me and chop me up in little pieces right here, who would know? The thought of it gives her an odd feeling of satisfaction, a possible conclusion.

Or she could, of course, be the one who kills him?

"Would you like me to show you the rest of the apartment?" he asks. "Or would you prefer to take a look at it on your own?"

"I would very much like you to show me around," she quickly says.

He guides her through the apartment, shows her the rooms, the big bedroom, the children's rooms, the office. He deliberately leaves the kitchen, the heart of the apartment, for last. That is where one ends up spending most of one's time, he explains to her, the view across the lawn, the towers and the lake, the precious types of wood that have been used for the surface of the table top, the expensive kitchen units, the American refrigerator, the dining table made by a cabinet maker which can be included in the price, the scullery in the next room, everything thoroughly done and utterly practical. She gets his whole little speech but basically doesn't respond to it. It's seldom that he doesn't manage to infect a potential customer with not even a tad of his enthusiasm but he can't make her out. He decides to hold back for a moment, turns around and looks at her.

She has removed her sunglasses and is standing stiff like a board staring into the scullery, as though she sees something in there that he can't. Her eyes are all shiny, a tear is trickling down her cheek. He takes a step toward her but decides to stop next to the stainless exhaust hood in the middle of the room. He considers telling her how much it cost but decides against it.

He can feel his telephone vibrating in his inner pocket but hopes she doesn't also sense it through the silence.

The Telephone

After a while a pattern became apparent, but you don't notice those things until you look back in retrospect. Every pattern first starts as a single point that develops into a line to later be incorporated in a regular structure if you look at it from a distance. A single point can't consist of the entire pattern, the first call is just a coincidence.

To begin with he didn't notice it, it was just the telephone ringing, someone who had called the wrong number and subsequently hung up. That didn't necessarily mean that anyone had to die, were dangling from a tree in the forest, blue in the face and with swollen limbs?

He is fifteen years old, standing with the receiver in his hand. That was back when there were telephone receivers and the telephone was attached to the wall with a wire.

On the other end of it he can hear someone breathing heavily and hanging up.

The episode is repeated several times the following days and it is irritating but nothing more than that. It could be someone from school, he thinks, a coincidence, something wrong with the telephone. It could be many things, sometimes he waits before hanging up but the heavy breathing just continues on the other end, heavy, like a child who has called the wrong number by accident and doesn't dare reveal who he is or hang up.

Not until he discovers that the call always comes when he's alone does the fear truly begin to settle in. It's always certain: His mother has just gone out shopping, his siblings downtown to the public swimming pool or to visit some friends. It becomes increasingly conspicuous, no sooner have they left than the heavy breather is sure to make his phone call.

And there he stands, holding the receiver in the big room and doesn't know what to do. Dust motes dance in a ray of sunshine from the window, surrounding the fireplace are ashes and small pieces of tile, a small geranium impregnates the air with its pungent scent of chewing gum. Right outside the window some chicks are making a lot of noise, you can tell when the parents return home to them with food, the sound of their scratching claws against the roof, the infernal chirping as the chicks fight for a bite of the worm. The heavy breathing through the receiver continues.

"This isn't funny anymore," he attempts, but apparently it is because the caller doesn't hang up the receiver, perhaps the breathing grows more rapid, clearer, interested, he can't tell for sure, but it continues to be there, in the receiver, just like the calls don't stop, on the contrary, they become more frequent.

He tries hanging up quickly, but then the phone rings immediately afterward, he doesn't pick it up, but it continues, he unplugs the telephone but that just makes it more frightening. The inaudible possibility that the telephone is ringing.

And gradually the house begins to change, the color nuances, the mood, his Adrenalin level. From experiencing an afternoon that was full of possibilities all its limitations now suddenly seem to emerge from the shadows. He can sit for several hours, frozen on the flowered couch in order to avoid making any sounds, at an angle where he can't be seen from the windows, and even though he has to go to the bathroom he doesn't dare go and doesn't dare admit to himself that he doesn't dare.

Being home alone goes from being fun to being a relief to hear the door being unlocked. He doesn't feel like telling his family about the calls because that would sound paranoid and self-absorbed and who wants to be any of those things? Who would spend their time keeping an eye on a fifteen year-old and breathe him heavily into his ear?

*

They live on a quiet residential road close to the water and across from it is where the expensive villas are situated with their beach properties. They don't take much interest in one another when they pass each other on the road, but greet one another and mind their own business, talk across the fence if it is urgent or they need to borrow a garden tool, like a milling machine or a lawn edge trimmer, for example. Their house is big and ocher yellow and is situated on a corner lot wedged between two roads. In the garden there are apple trees and a big copper beech he can see from his basement window.

Their neighbor is in the accounting business, drives an Opel and wears a light gray suit and always has a dark brown attaché case tucked under his arm. Across the street lives a woman who is a former member of parliament and whose voice pierces through all the niceness of the neighborhood like a knife that cuts through butter, or perhaps rather a circular saw through gravel. You can hear her long before you see her as she shouts the day's program to her grandchildren whom she sometimes watches. Noise and chaos follow her wherever she goes. She drives her car, a rusty Nissan, at the maximum shift and slips in the clutch much too fast, making the cogwheels screech; she slams doors and shouts her greetings across the hedge. Next to her, diagonally opposite, live the pilot and his wife, a well-kept lady in her forties, tailor-made suit, silk scarves and hairstyles done by hairstylists. The pilot himself is seldom seen, he flies overseas and only returns home every once in a while in his white uniform with its gilt borders at the sleeves. He lifts his cap in greeting if anyone happens to be outside as he waits for the gate to open so that he can park his convertible English sports car in the garage. When he is home they go out to eat and the wife beams, she is finally being rewarded for the many hours she has sacrificed in order to maintain her looks while he was in Australia, USA, Kenya.

Those who are particularly observant will notice the gift right away, usually a new scarf, but it can also be a piece of jewelry: a twisted gold chain or a pair of earrings with emerald green stones.

A little further down the road lives a dainty old lady who wears earth-colored clothes and whom he helps take care of the garden, and a family with children whom they don't like for various reasons.

*

All summer they sit out on the little terrace facing the water. Like now. They have just been down to the beach in their bare feet and are now sitting at the round table drinking tea, eating toasted soft rolls with Tilsit-type cheese and orange marmalade. He is wearing his mother's old brown bathrobe, the others have changed to their summer clothes while he has set the table.

His sister is the first to hear it.

"Shhh" she says dramatically, putting her finger to her lips. She wants to be an actress, is secretly in love with Anthony Andrews and wants to study drama at the same school he did in Scotland.

"Can't you hear it?"

In the silence they hear an unpleasant, lamenting sound. An animal in difficulty? If she doesn't become an actress she wants to become a vet.

"Could it be a cat?" he asks.

His mother shakes her head and gets up, tries to perceive where the sound is coming from and walks out to the road. The others follow her, perhaps in order to protect her should it turn out to be dangerous, an injured alien with a laser rifle, for example. The sound is definitely inhuman, mechanical and bestial all at once. It's coming from the pilot's property, and his mother is already making her way across the street. She enters through the parking lot and behind the hedge. They can hear her say something and the lamenting sound transforms into a whimper, like that of a child who has cried for so long that it can't stop. They can hear the sound of a woman's voice who is trying to explain something between the whimpers, his mother, who is answering it consolingly.

"It was just an unhappy woman," says his mother when she returns. "I think I got her to calm down, poor little thing."

Something about her husband's been cheating on her, the pilot's been having affairs with the stewardesses while he's been away on his long trips, how cliché-like can you get? She is practically being devoured by her jealousy once she has started getting suspicious. It has grown big and sits on her shoulders like a dragon. That was her image, not mine. She thinks everyone knows it, she hardly dares budge from her plot but at home she constantly finds new evidence: telephone numbers, blond hair, lipstick marks, the scent of perfume she doesn't recognize.

"I invited her over for tea but she said she needed more to rest." his mother looks at her watch and goes inside and fetches the car keys. She has to go to the hairdresser's, his sister rides along with her to the station.

After they've driven off the phone rings.

*

After that their view of the pilot changes. They continue to greet him when he returns home in his sports car but where they used to think of it as cool, the whole thing with his overnight bag, white uniform and gold stripes, they now have a different opinion about all of that.

His mother wants to give him a piece of her mind about responsibility and morals, but his father forbids her to do it and several weeks will pass before she gets a sort of opportunity to do so.

Meanwhile the calls continue and one afternoon while he is sitting in his basement room he suddenly hears a melody, a simple melody from a music box. He is home alone and is for once not listening to music. It must be a car that drove past or a boy out on the street he forces himself to think. He concentrates on his homework but when the melody returns there can no longer be any doubt. The melody is coming from the yard just outside the window. Somebody must be down on their knees out there churning a small handle, and he runs through the basement and up the stairs and into the yard but the individual is, of course, gone by that time.

And not until then does he notice that he is shaking all over, that his heart is pounding against his chest, that he is on the verge of tears. Not because he is afraid, I think, but because he is afraid that he is going mad.

*

A few days later they get to ride with the pilot. His mother meets him out on the street and this time he is the one who is beside himself. They apparently take turns with that. His wife is gone and she has left a letter that makes him feel apprehensive. He is sitting on the terrace but comes out to them when he hears my mother's voice.

"She wrote that I could find her up by the lake at Kobberdammen. The place where we ate lunch right after we were married." He says it in an odd, monotonous tone of voice, as though he isn't fully present but reading some lines out loud he once wrote down. He walks back and forth on the road in his loafers, faintly whimpering to himself, what have I done?

"You've broken her heart, that's what you've done," his mother says. The pilot gives her a transparent look.

"Come on, we have to go find her before she does something rash." He nods, walks like a marionette doll over to his car that for once is parked out on the street. "

"Are you able to drive?" his mother asks and he nods once more. For some reason or other it seems natural for them to ride along. As though they have suddenly become friends. His mother doesn't want to let him drive alone and she nods for him to get in. She gets in the front seat next to the pilot and he squeezes into the microscopic back seat.

The pilot sobs softly all the way up there, his mother tries to console him but of course manages to weave in a few moral admonitions, "You should have thought about that a little earlier."

They park the car and walk into the forest. The gravel crunches under their feet, he shouts, "Kamilla!" and his voice echoes among the tree trunks. He starts running away from the path, through the leaves that are lying, brown, on the forest floor, even though it is summer, he stumbles over some branches but gets back on his feet and staggers down to the lake. He disappears behind a hill and they follow him. There is only their footsteps, the chirping of some invisible birds, the wind among the leaves.

Nature doesn't seem to care.

They hear him before they see him. A bestial scream, then some loud shouts, weeping. His mother starts to run.

"Stay here," she says.

*

She has arranged a picnic under a big tree down by the edge of the lake. She has spread out a red chequered blanket and placed plates and glasses on it, napkins, a bottle of champagne. In the middle is a picnic basket from which a baguette is sticking out, a carton of milk and a sausage. Above the blanket she is hanging dressed in a blue dress he has never seen before, her hair done up and her feet bare. A distance away from the blanket there are a pair of lacquered shoes and next to them the pilot is sitting and crying in a ray of sunshine that has struggled its way through the canopy of leaves.

He stares at the pilot's wife, until the image has engraved itself in his memory, an image of sorrow, meaninglessness and transitoriness that would never leave him. Her face is blue-black, her eyes staring empty into space and her legs have become swollen. The pilot must have pushed her because she is spinning round herself in a last waltz before the grave.

Maybe it's the wind.

His mother comes over to shield him from the image. She embraces him clumsily and pushes him practically back up toward the parking lot. She gets someone to promise to call the police before she drags him with her to the bus stop. For some reason or other she goes into the bakery right across the street and buys two raspberry cookies. She doesn't say anything and they eat the cookies in silence as they wait for the bus, sitting on the bench in the green shelter and rustling with the bags. Some children pass them carrying big schoolbags on their backs, an older man tiptoes across the road dressed in a robe in the direction of the water.

At some point the bus must have come, he doesn't remember it, but to this very day he associates the taste of raspberry cookies with death. Death is sweet and sticky, that's what he learned that day; the day the calls stopped.

The Vixen Man

Today there are very few who speak with him. When he goes shopping he can sense how people talk about him behind his back, pull their children a little away, turn their backs to him. Maybe it's something he's imagining. He fills his basket with items, canned sausages, toilet paper, whole grain bread and walks down through the aisles without stopping. He knows what he's going to buy, so there's no reason for him to compare any of the items, read the label of contents or look at the prices. He isn't driven by his impulses. Had it been an electronics store it would probably have been a different story, he is crazy about electronic devices, most anything that can be plugged into a socket interests him. In a way that's part of the problem, where the whole thing got started.

No, his chickens disappeared, one after another, that was how it all started. The chickens disappeared and he was convinced that it had been the neighbor's dog that had taken them, a big, wire-haired chicken-dog, you would have thought it would have been a simple matter of pleading guilty. The dog was always running around in the yard, barking at birds, at strangers, from happiness. Of course the dog was the one who would run into his yard every so often and grab a chicken. Once he had almost caught it red-handed, it had been running after a ball in his yard but quickly rushed back with its tail between its legs when he shouted at it. Maybe he had also thrown a single rock, at least that's what the neighbor claimed later, he couldn't remember it anymore.

He didn't have a particularly close relationship with his neighbor, but they were far from enemies. Or: they weren't back then. They didn't eat dinner together or bring one another leftover cake, never asked for anything (sugar, tools, walking the dog), but they would greet one another if they happened to be passing by and saw the other one in his yard.

The neighbor worked at an advertising agency. Såsæd was its name. He had previously been part of a spiritual community on Lolland, now he was selling hot air to private companies instead. He had made a few ad campaigns for the local private school, for the feedstuff factory and the furniture shop on Storegade. He had a beard, sometimes he practiced tai-chi on his front lawn.

*

He was very fond of his chickens, gave them names, spoke with them, remembered to feed them and give them water on the hour. He didn't think he was in any way fanatic about his poultry keeping, but they meant something to him, his chickens, after Ingrid left him a few years ago they had grown to become his closest companions. Aside from the eggs, they provided him with a sense of intimacy and he provided them with a safe environment. Something for something.

He spent some time collecting himself before letting his neighbor in on his suspicions. He had carefully thought through how he was going to present the problem, in an impartial, neutral way and with a grain of forthcoming humor, but his neighbor flatly rejected him. His dog would never do a thing like that, he said, it was a kind and affectionate dog, not a killer. Furthermore, it never left their property.

"Now that's not true," said the man. "I've seen it over here several times."

"I don't believe it, it would never go outside the fence." His neighbor spoke in a gentle, overbearing tone of voice so that you hardly noticed just how confrontational his words actually were. He had been prepared for that.

"It's in the dog's nature to take chickens," he said, " it doesn't mean that it's malicious, it just means it's an animal." He thought he had composed himself rather well. He mostly felt like swinging his fist right up in the face of that holier-than -thou idiot, but he chose to argue his case instead.

"But it doesn't have it in him, you've gotta understand that, I know that dog," the neighbor said.

"I'd still like for you to keep it on a leash or make a kennel for it, if it has to be outside."

"That's never going to happen. Perhaps then I should ask you to put a muzzle on your rooster. I haven't asked you to do that even though I hadn't foreseen having a chicken farm as our neighbor when I moved to the city."

The part about the city was quite a misrepresentation on his part but he didn't take it back. 197 people lived in Vindinge, his house was the last before the town sign, on the other side of it were fields for as long as the eye could see.

*

He decided to put up a fight and did the only thing he could: he drove to the electronic shop in the mall where he bought infra-red outdoor cameras with sensors , a new server, two screens and an HD recorder. He installed the entire thing when he came home, the cameras, so that they monitored the entire chicken farm and parts of the yard and the server and the screens in the scullery. If there was any movement outside the fence the recorder would begin of its own accord, but he still ended up spending a lot of time in front of the two screens the coming nights. He was looking forward to getting the damning piece of evidence against his neighbor's dirty dog recorded and he was particularly looking forward to going over to his neighbor's with a DVD of HD quality. He already knew what he intended to say. He wouldn't gloat, but he wanted his revenge.

On the fourth night the evidence arose. He had gone out to let out the chickens and immediately noticed that one was missing. There were traces left over from a fight: there was a trail of blood and feathers from the chicken house to the fence which the dog had managed to dig himself under. A feeling of sorrow mixed with triumph spread through his body and he rushed inside to fetch the DVD. He watched the recording from the previous night over breakfast, homemade rolls with cheese and black coffee, and ten minutes into it the culprit appeared. Once again, he was mesmerized by the high quality of the recording, the picture was razor-sharp even though it was twilight. He started when he saw something moving at the neighbor's property line, some branches were bent to the side, some leaves rustled.

Finally, he thought, finally!

And then he was left with a sense of disappointment and coffee breath, a half-finished roll and a picture of a fox. It carefully stuck its head out between the branches at the property line and at first he couldn't see what it was, its head had the same size as the dog's, but when it moved on the grass there was no longer any doubt. The quality of the recording was as good as watching Discovery Channel, it was clearly a fox. It dug its way under the fence in a matter of no time, found a crack in the house and shortly afterward came out carrying a chicken in its mouth. It stopped before squeezing itself underneath the fence, sniffed a little in the air, as though it could hear something and stared for a brief moment into one of the cameras. He put the recording on pause at that point. The fox's gaze toward his own, and tried to understand, tried to work through what had actually taken place to get it to match his own inner visions.

He slowly went out to the hallway and took down his jacket from the hook, opened the door as had he been in a trance, at least his eyes were empty and his movements mechanical. He himself didn't know why he was acting like that, but apparently he knew that he had to go out.

He went for a long walk in the city, along the road down toward the thicket. It was turning into autumn, most of the leaves were still hanging on the trees but they were getting ready to let go and there was a fresh breeze without any trace left of the summer. He walked past Madsen's cows that were grazing a little inside the field and he could hear a bird of prey shrieking somewhere above him.

When he returned he took out an old fox trap from the shed. He checked it, tested it and set it up right outside the hole under the fence, camouflaged it with leaves and grass, went inside and put up some water for a for a coffee punch.

*

No one except the fox man knows how the chicken dog ended up in the fox trap. But naturally people drew their own conclusions and they were helped along the way by the neighbor who told his version of the story just as eagerly as he would have told about Sofa-Møller's outstanding qualities. In his mind there wasn't a shadow of a doubt that it had been the neighbor who had caught his dog and forced it into the trap.

The dog had to be put down, the bones in one of its forelegs had been crushed, its paw dangling from just a few threads when he finally managed to get it free. Furthermore, the dog had fallen at such an unfortunate angle that it had broken its thigh. After a day of searching for it, he finally found it lying on the ground with its eyes shut and whimpering. There was no trace of the neighbor, on the other hand. He had taken his jacket and had left and hadn't returned until several days later, a group of children had seen him outside of town. He looked like a vagabond.

*

Since then the fox-man hasn't felt compelled to defend himself, but meets people's gaze when he shops at the grocery for toilet paper, whole grain bread, sometimes honey and Coco-Pops. He rushes through the store without looking down, pushes the shopping cart out to the car and drives the usual route back home. At home he reads encyclopedia entries. He can barely remember how it began, on sale in the antique store, but now he is determined to read the entire humongous encyclopedia from start to finish. He has reached the letter "m"... "m" as in malicious, "m" as in mistrustful, "m" as in Mikhail.

Sometimes he watches his recordings at night. Less frequently now, but each time it gives him an odd sense of satisfaction, knowing that he is the only who knows what happened that night, that he is the only one who knows the true version of the story. And then the quality of the recordings, they were truly unsurpassed.

Mikhail

Mikhail Sergejevich Gorbachev (Russian: Михаил Сергéевич Горбачёв) (born March 2, 1931) was a very erotic individual, not many people know that. Whenever he was alone he would take off his clothes and dance around in his house, from the bedroom to the kitchen, from the guest bathroom to the hallway, there wasn't a spot that his bare feet left untouched. Already as a young man in Stavropol he would dance, as a member of the police bureau in Moscow, and perhaps specifically in the villa facing the Black Sea on Crimea where he was later held under house arrest for three days as the Soviet Union dissolved.

"Look, I'm dancing, " he said to Raisa.

"Hmm", said Raisa.

"This is how you dance, Raisa!" he cheered as his rather large reproductive organ swung in time with his supple thighs. Sometimes he would also put on music but that wasn't a prerequisite for the dancing, he listened to music even when it wasn't there, he felt it in his body through the silence.

He remembered even more clearly when he met Raisa; how the day tasted, how the air felt, how her skin felt (like a ripe plum). He discovered her for the first time at a lecture on agriculture at the university in Moscow, something about reforming agricultural methods, he wasn't listening because her pale neck took up all his attention, her wild, red hair, her cheek that rounded when she smiled (he sat two rows behind her). Later that same evening they met, apparently by accident, at the ball in the ballroom, and they danced; he caressed her back, her behind during the dance, plucked up his courage and removed a sweaty strand of hair from her cheek.

Later they kissed.

Gorbachev wrote down some details from their first encounter in his diary which he recorded with a particular zealous interest for all things sensual throughout his life. It is actually possible to piece together a kind of erotic manifest from it. Most of it consists of sentences taken out of context, snapshots caught in solidified ink on the yellowing parchment, others are brief reflections: a pendant dangling between the breasts of a young girl, the reflection of a face in a train window one dark night; soft voices, usually Norwegian; the way in which women play with their hair, the way they arrange it in a bun in the back of their neck with rehearsed movements as though they could reveal the secrets of the female sex if they fumbled; self-confident women (wearing tight jeans); a well-shaped thigh, tanned by the sun and semi-covered by a loose, often white dress, biking. And now that he thought about it: curves in general, the curves of the ass (for lack of a less vulgar word), of the breast, the curvature of the back. He was reminded of a comment that was made at a committee meeting that had taken him completely aback, a teasing glance across the table, so he was forced to shyly lower his eyes, like a schoolboy. If he had to name his favorite spot on a woman's body, a part that he could take with him to a deserted island, he would have chosen Raisa's dimples right above her buttocks.

This erotic aspect arises, he once wrote somewhere, when one encounters for the first time that which one desires but can't get. The burning gaze, the encouraging smile from a passing girl, the thought of what could happen (in contrast to pornography where everything actually did happen). He could still remember what it felt like as a young man to follow the girls in Stavropol, trying to catch a scent, a fleeting glance; the physical satisfaction of fearfully stealing a glance at a beautiful woman's breast, only to, with his heart pounding and on the verge of fainting, turn down a side alley.

With Raisa all of that changed. Now it was sufficient to look at her neck when she sat with her back to him in the green easy chair, bathed in the sleepy light from a Chinese lamp. The knowledge that she was his, that he had the right to gently stroke her hair, that she could embrace him with her hands awkwardly above her head, turn smiling ; that she could remove their clothes, both his and hers, kiss his beauty mark; that they could lie naked together, her soft body against his, her curvy breast which he was allowed to caress.

Afterward he could dance through the house naked, from the bedroom to the kitchen, from the guest bathroom to the hallway.

Some time afterward Raisa's death he attempted a careful dance without any audience. He undressed and danced a few steps experimentally around the living room; the soft, hand-knotted carpet underneath his toes, the dull yellow glow of the standing lamp, the mild scent of autumn. It seemed right but didn't really work and when he saw his reflection in the dark window panes facing the yard, he stopped, letting his arms fall to his sides and gave up.

Today he runs his own private consulting firm in Moscow.

The Water

It's as though it all comes pouring in and he thinks, "Let it gush in." He is standing in the shower where the warm jets of water hit his naked skin and it's as though they're the ones who make it all gush inside of him, all around him, in a long, descending movement, it collapses, and he lets it collapse, laughs out loud, sits down in the shower stall as the jets of water drum a mad melody on his trembling body until he gives it a language after all, thinking: So then I collapsed in the shower, lay on the floor laughing, retell what is occurring as it occurs and then it no longer collapses, collects itself, the shower is just a shower, the jets of water merely just water coming out of a calcified shower head.

He tries to let go again, to retrace his steps back to the madness, but now it's all language, it's all taking place inside his mind; the water, the jets, his laughing. Follow it, he thinks, at the heels of falling normality, and he manages to slow down the pace, to observe the dissolution in slow motion, the drops that leave the shower and approach his face, caught in their descent by his gaze, like the water in a waterfall that you follow from the top toward the river below. The water vapour that rises from the floor hangs in a cloud in front of the shower cubicle, steams up the mirror, gushes forth from the crack under the door, making a German family shriek and wrap their raincoats around them, the trees already glistening from the moisture, the monkeys screaming and disappearing up into the treetops with long, nonchalant movements. One of them snatches the camera from the hand of the German woman, sits at a meter's distance away from her and amuses himself by holding it up and puckering his lips.The woman turns toward her husband, she no longer sees the comical aspect of the situation, suddenly she feels as though the whole world is watching her and that it is no longer just a monkey with a camera, but it is about what is yours and mine and the desire to be anonymous, a deserted island, a hunting lodge somewhere in Sweden where the fire is crackling in the fireplace and the husband is out most of the day. He smiles back and shrugs his shoulders because what had she expected him to do, catch the monkey, which has in the meantime turned its red behind toward them and disappeared into the hallway, down the stairs, still semi-enshrouded by the dampness from the bath. Screams can be heard down there, his daughters', his wife's, something that topples over, a child's hysterical weeping, his wife's soothing voice.

He smiles. He smiles and dries himself in a large towel, puts on his clothes using violent movements, runs his hand through his wet hair, walks down the stairs. He stops in front of the door to the living room from which tumultuous sounds can still be heard, reaches for the doorknob, but changes his mind, stands for a moment with his hand extended in the air, takes instead his raincoat from the coat hook, a sudden impulse, slings it across his shoulder and walks out.

*

He walks down the road, one foot in front of the other in a rhythm that spreads through the rest of his body, like the beating of the heart, first one, then the next, the same rhythm, and the waterproof material of the coat that makes a pleasant swishing sound for every step he takes. So here I am walking, he thinks as he looks around at the houses he passes, practical houses fenced in by hedges or lath fences, bricks, gutters, windows cemented in by a Polish bricklayer's apprentice who was brought here by a bigger company that offered him a container and good companionship, Danish open faced sandwiches and beer in the weekends.

He spreads out his arms and welcomes the rain that is falling down harder now. Water, water, madness, he smiles, the delightful madness, its essence and derivation. He looks at his watch, turns his left hand up, making the sleeves fall back, crosses the road to the station, goes in through the double doors, up the staircase to the platform. He can hear the train rumbling above him and he is running, one foot quickly lifted above the other like two drum sticks, the manic swishing sound of the coat, the shortness of his breath, the fear of the sound of the whistle of departure. Fumbles for his train card, manages to check in, stumbling through door just before it closes.

He finds a seat and looks around among the gray suits, freshly ironed shirts, expensive briefcases, shaven faces, the scent of eau de cologne, a single child who is tiredly leaning against his father who is busy reading a newspaper. He looks out at the houses and at the rain hitting the window pane in drops that run backward in horizontal lines. He leans his head against the cold glass pane, his eyes follow a raindrop that is dancing backward in a quiver, but then the rain intensifies as though someone had turned on a water faucet and he looks up at the sky, almost expecting to see the shower head but only sees the dark clouds that reach all the way down to the ground, the water that is coming down in buckets, in cascades against the window pane, a regular waterfall that drowns out everything, the beating of his heart, the crumpling of the newspapers, the humming of the train. He looks up and suddenly everyone looks more tired than they did a minute ago, their gray faces and he and he concludes (sensibly) that it is the light or the darkness, the clouds that have stolen the sun, but he squints and the gray faces become distorted as well. The eyes of the girl, for example, are completely askew, cheering fretfully. Her father turns around, scowling, with yellow eyes and a deformed chin which just a moment ago was nicely shaped and newly shaven. He puts down his newspaper, smiles at his daughter, points and suddenly the train is teeming with idiots whose ramblings are drowned out by the sound of the rain. He can see that it has already drowned out the railway line, that the water outside is rising, penetrating leaky cracks in the train.

A disfigured man tears at himself until he starts bleeding right in front of him, another one pushes his eyes into his sockets with a silent scream, another is busy consuming a garbage bag but throws it all up before he manages to finish it all, yellow bile is floating in the aisle and the stench of it spreads, not just of bile but of pus, and madness. In a way he is relieved when the roof of the train falls off and the fresh air that enters removes the stench and the rain washes the floor clean. They are no longer riding on tracks, he notices, they are drifting with the current. On the other hand, the rain has died down, the train engineer has gotten up in the very back of the carriage and is trying to steer the train with a pole. Several of the imbeciles assist him, hanging cheerfully over the side of the barge, pulling magazines through the water in long hauls so that water is pouring down their sleeves.

Apparently they are no longer going to Vanløse.

He puts up his feet on the seat across from him and leans back. That wasn't what he had been expecting, but it almost couldn't have been any different. A small barge floats by and he waves resignedly. Some idiots throw a garland up into the air, sob when they see it hit the water behind the barge, flowing with the current behind them.

The Boat

The water comes from Tibet. I can feel it when I put my hand into it; the dreamy sensation of Tintin in driving snow and mountain summits that melt, streaming down the mountain sides to later collect into one stream that continues to run toward me and from there southward, only now with this boat and this "I" balancing on his invisible hands, my hand, dancing on the swell, my gaze that disappears in the eddy, my own self in apathetic calmness down the river. There is nothing more calming than a landscape in motion, than streaming water in eternal transformation, suddenly all you can do is stare, or: finally, all you can do is stare, finally one is a little more satisfied than indifferent.

The boat is filled to the brim, and this is where it all begins. It should perhaps have appeared earlier, but here it is. So lets start all over: it doesn't start with a street entertainer, not with a chubby editor, my god, that's definitely not where it started. That's where it all ends, I must have turned it upside down and now that I'm taking a closer look at it, doesn't it all look slightly inverted?

So in other words, it begins on a lake in Laos, with a full boat that is being carried by the stream. It also has an engine (how could I forget that?) that makes such an infernal racket in the back that it practically drowns out a group of young travelers who have been drinking beer ever since we left yesterday. Now they stand shouting their arguments and anecdotes in the eternal competition of who has traveled the longest in the most genuine way, seen the most authentic things.

I have, no doubt about that, but I remain silent on my plastic seat as I make do with scowling toward the noise as a forgetful part of me longs to be just as young, inexperienced and receptive. And without gravitas. In their own minds they are big and strong, with full grown beards and muscles for travel, but their beards are wispy and soft, their stomachs unbearably flat, and if anything they look like birds, cranes on thin legs, clumsy and conceited, in an eternal and ungracious mating dance with the girls traveling with them, life, themselves. They will never be wiser than they are right now, at this very moment, but nothing can make them understand that, and who wouldn't mind casting off twenty pounds, twenty years, and sit down, skinny and stupid, next to them and tell them about all the cool places one has been to while drinking beer and simultaneously trying to score the anorectic German who, sullen and nougat-brown, sits looking indifferently across the provisional bar counter?

The boat is a flat-bottomed barge with a homemade canopy made of planks and driftwood, that was where we came from. It's not the kind you cast wreaths after, not the kind you sing melancholic songs to. It's the kind you use to drift down the river noisily. There are four centimeters from the paddock to the surface of the water, the tarpaulin to keep the water out when things get out of hand. Oh yes, and to keep the sun out. It's 40 degrees and here and there are small pools of sweat on the plastic seats when people get up and take a restless walk through the middle deck.

*

The riverside is a bottomless mixture of mud and slag in which you can sink to your knees as you stand looking across the river waiting for the ships to sail by. An endless row of naked children have done just that since we left land. When they catch sight of the boat they shout to their friends who then come running from behind the trees, down the slopes, down toward the river where they jump up and down, shouting to us in their small, shrill voices.

It was here the real colonel Kurtz carried on, somewhere there in the jungle. Tony Poe, another fat American with a weakness for alcohol and severed heads, a bald crown, and always in the mud-built shadow with a hand over his sweaty head. He became known for rewarding soldiers for cutting off the ears of their enemies. He would send them to the American embassy in Vientiane as proof of his belligerent dedication and diligence but unfortunately a secretary became so sick from the stench of the rotten flesh that he, for her sake, stopped doing it. Perhaps also because his soldiers began cutting off their own ears and one another's in order to get the five thousand offered tips. and even though those earless soldiers looked funny it also seemed somewhat demoralizing when the money had been spent on three packs of cigarettes and a blow job. So instead they started severing the entire heads off their enemies to later hurl them from planes above their surviving friends. Or they would put them on sticks to horrify their enemies and amuse themselves.

*

You get a strange sense of destiny when sitting in a flat-bottomed barge, the river binds us together in a pact of equal portions of fear for the unknown surrounding us, for the hidden dangers of the water, for the cerebrospinal meningitis the mosquitoes are carrying and typhus. Those confounded mosquitoes that swarm in the boat and around our sweaty faces when the darkness begins to transition to twilight, then we move imperceptibly closer together, become tolerant of one another's crooked stories that we suddenly feel the urge to share with one another in a mood of loss and catharsis before the approaching deliverance.

In the morning we look at one another shyly.

I'm sitting next to a thin-haired British guy who is covering his mouth with one of his hands as he speaks as though to feign a shyness that doesn't really match the words that slip past his hand and through the cracks between his skinny-boned fingers. He laughs out loud at his own mischiefs. He knows numerous stories from the tropics, about aid workers, beggars and prostitutes, one story replacing the other in a long chain. And he shares them gladly, you can discern a smile behind his hand.

"My sister is a porn actress. That's not how she presents herself but I've seen one of her films. Bad lighting and no plot, but she has a big pair of breasts, you've gotta give her that. It was my father who gave them to her. As a repentance."

"As a repentance for what?"

He looks at me with an empty gaze.

"Yes, well, it was a poor investment. Right now he is dying in his country house and none of us care to see him. Not even now, after the breasts. It's ironic."

He gets up to buy a beer. I follow him.

"I'll go home when he is dead and not a second earlier."

Sitting on the other side of the aisle is the pilot whose wife committed suicide in a forest in Northern Zealand. The Brit pats him on the shoulder as we pass, nods to the pilgrim who bicycled from Jerusalem after having received a visit from Jesus in his apartment. I got the story yesterday, it wasn't coherent, but, then again, neither is the man, his skin is chapped and he has lost most of his hair and his stomach is hanging out above his belt. I stop and comment on the colorful book he is reading as the Brit continues up to the bar where he hands some bills across the counter. He turns around and hands me one of the beers once I reach him. He's already started conversing with a black-haired woman who's wearing sunglasses. I stand a little bit off to the side. One of the loud youths is trying to communicate with me but gives up when I pull out a pocket edition of J.P Jacobsen's poems from my pocket and read, very concentrated, "Why life! Why death!" I can hear the girl with the sunglasses in a sniffling voice mention something to the Brit about a tyrannical father, a brother she lost contact with and he responds courteously, shares his story about his own father, enters the competition of neglect.

"South East Asia is a veritable haven for people who are trying to flee from themselves," I hear him say, and from others, from doubtful actions performed on the other side of the world but which wouldn't make anyone out here so much as lift an eyebrow. Everyone here encourages excessive behavior, to compare the sense of justice on the pretext of following the customs of the country, and the domestic moral budges an invisible bit day for day. In every back room you will find a fat European man with a beer, a remote and a skinny Thai girl on his cock. That's the norm, and who's going to deviate from that?

*

Time is what we have most of in the barge, stories are shared, there is flirting and drinking. Books are read about the places we sail through and about the places I'll be visiting afterward. Devotional reading about human maliciousness, about Pol Pot's terror regime, about the victims of the Khmer Rouge, about brainwash and blackmail. And as exotic trees, red cliffs and slopes float past us, screaming children and huts of straw, the images keep streaming through my mind. Wanton images of wives dangling above freshly-set picnic blankets, raspberry cakes, porno breasts, relief workers--and of a childhood friend who got a pile of rocks on his head thrown from the first floor. The image of the scarred top of his head the first time he removed his cap, the image of the bloody heads of my best friends slowly descending from the sky, the image of the young victims of the Khmer Rouge, of middle-aged white men with Thai girls sitting on their laps, on the back of a scooter, in their hand in a sallow hotel.

The water streaming, the days, the images, the stories, the morale.

When we have sailed far enough out the boat docks at a floating ponton which we poor river-fatigued souls stagger onto. Some small barges are docked to the sides, ready to sail us to the shore. Yet still it is almost unbearable having to wait any longer, the trance has been broken, impatience and the ordinary sense of time has taken over.

Our baggage is thrown into a pile and the Brit lifts his eyebrow and shakes his head with disdain when he sees his expensive weekend bag tumble down the heap. We try to make some small talk, but the trip is over, the pact has been dissolved. Now all we want is to move on, find a place where we can be ourselves, where we can stare into a wall, watch TV, masturbate in peace.

The pilgrim has found his backpack and is attempting to balance it into the boat as an older woman from Holte stands looking perplexedly at her own piece of luggage that a muscular Laotian is busy loading up front. I go over and help her down, give her arm a small squeeze on the way and she sends a grateful smile up at me.

The Brit covers his mouth with his hand and mutters good-bye. We have agreed to meet at his resort in Thailand where the waves are meant for surfing, the sun always shines and the slender waitresses serve the best sushi in the country. That is also where two Danes who spend their winters there, live, I would like them, good hedonists, both of them.

He climbs down into the boat and waves up at me before the engine starts with a roar and transports them to the shore. I have to wait until the boats start returning to pick up the last passengers. But finally we set out and sail the twenty meters toward shore where the last of my co-passengers have collected all their baggage and are now busy spreading out in all directions from the dock out into the world.

My body feels completely heavy. Tired and dizzy. It is as though the red ground under me has given way, threatening to swallow me up.

Above me an eagle cries, a good distance from where I'm standing a figure in a strange costume is standing waving at me. I stare back at him apathetically. He lifts his hat. Then he takes a step forward, shouting " "Come closer, my friend, don't just stand there staring. Come and try to make a guess, win a fortune or lose yourself."

So that is where the whole thing began after all.

The Blow

The whole thing begins with a blow to the head. Later, in a little while, it will become apparent that it came from a bottle that someone has presumably swung, but that plays no role right now. All I feel is the blow and just barely, not the hard fall on the sidewalk, not my legs bent under me in an impossible angle, I sense that I am opening my eyes, with a single stroke of the eyelids, reasoning backward, the fall, the blow, the bottle. That is where we are at. It rolls away from me, the sound of glass against concrete, pieces of broken glass, some distance away a pair of legs that disappear with quick steps, gray pants, sensible shoes.

Things are turning, the concrete, the bottle, the world or: me. I turn to the side, get up with my elbow against the ground, the clouds above my head, but also an advertising sign with an "m" , voices a distance down the road. Why?

Elephants are the only animals who have four knees and no elbows! Elephants are the only animals, the only clouds, woolly tufts of steam, custom-tailored snow. I must have tumbled on my back, and here come the pains, the pains and the bottle that has ended its impossible circular tour without end, it rolls toward me ever so slowly. As though it is asking for good weather, as though it is kissing my ribs, as though it is apologizing. As though.

It is sailing.

Glimpses of happiness. Of joy. A glimpse of summer.

In other words: It was a bottle, at the end of the bottle a hand, at the end of the hand an arm, a torso, a man. Sensible shoes, gray pants. Hunched shoulders?

Now I'm guessing.

I'm trying to sit up, turn around again on my side, push off. there is an arm that helps me, a voice? I am alone, but an arm helped me, a voice. That made a sound? I don't understand a thing, they fall apart: all the things. The more you understand.

The more you understand, the wiser you get. The wiser you get, the harder life becomes.

That's how you sit.

That's how you kneel.

That's how you stand.

And that's how you stagger along the street after your murderer, out of the story.

Kristian Himmelstrup (www.himmelstrup.info) has an M.A. from both The University of Washington and The University of Copenhagen and has taught language, cultural studies and creative writing at universities in Denmark and the US. He made his debut in 2004 with the novel *Last Tango of the Dinosaur* and has since published further two novels and a collection of short stories along with several books on literature and cultural studies.

Nina Sokol is a poet and translator in the midst of translating novels, short stories. plays and poems by Danish writers. She was a grant poet-in-residence at The Vermont Studio Center in 2011. She has received several grants from the Danish Art's Council to translate plays, including a play written by the fairy tale writer H.C. Andersen which was published by the journal "InTranslation." She has also translated an excerpt from one of the winning novels of last year›s EU Prize for Literature (Danish, 2016) as well as translated such authors Niviaq Korneliussen and Bjørn Rasmussen. Her own poems have appeared in American journals, including *Miller's Pond* and the *Hiram Poetry Review* and a collection was published by Lapwing Publications in Belfast, Ireland (2015).

www.ingramcontent.com/pod-product-compliance
Lightning Source LLC
Chambersburg PA
CBHW050538190726
48284CB00003B/1126

9 781952 419010